Bitter Honey

Also by Caryl Lewis

Drift

CARYL LEWIS

BITTER HONEY

doubleday

TRANSWORLD PUBLISHERS

UK | USA | Canada | Ireland | Australia
India | New Zealand | South Africa

Transworld is part of the Penguin Random House group of companies
whose addresses can be found at global.penguinrandomhouse.com

Penguin Random House UK,
One Embassy Gardens, 8 Viaduct Gardens, London SW11 7BW

penguin.co.uk

Penguin
Random House
UK

First published in Great Britain in 2025 by Doubleday
an imprint of Transworld Publishers

1

Typeset in 12.75/16 pt Granjon by Falcon Oast Graphic Art Ltd.
Printed and bound in Great Britain by Clays Ltd, Elcograf S.p.A.

The authorized representative in the EEA is Penguin Random House Ireland,
Morrison Chambers, 32 Nassau Street, Dublin D02 YH68.

A CIP catalogue record for this book is available from the British Library

ISBN 9780857527899

Penguin Random House is committed to a sustainable
future for our business, our readers and our planet. This book is
made from Forest Stewardship Council® certified paper.

For A. R. Hughes
Let us not miss each other

A seed in the heart of an apple is an orchard invisible

Old Welsh Proverb

I feel tremulous, Hannah, vulnerable to the slightest tug of the wintering winds. These last few weeks, I've felt myself detach so much from the world that I can sense my own falling, my slow drifting to earth. All these years, I've indulged myself with the illusion of for ever, and still, even now, on waking or as we eat breakfast in a comfortable silence, I glimpse it, like the azure flicker of a jay's wing through the orchard. That pretence of permanence. That necessary fickle glint of light that allows us to live on, to not be driven mad.

You know that language is leaving me, too. I look for the words my mother gave me, but they are not there, which leads me daily into abyss after abyss after abyss. The connections between words and their meaning are loosening, also, as if the map of my mind is disintegrating, yet old names and places now long gone come back to me uninvited. The strangest thing is that time itself has changed for me. The stories of all my yesterdays now show through my threadbare todays and, as we both know, I cannot possibly have many tomorrows. Perhaps I should be grateful – the only privilege, it seems, of teetering on the edge is feeling for the first time free from time.

The words I collected for my books have gone now, their work with me done. The relentlessness with which they plagued me, preoccupied me, the

*way they kept me awake and cluttered my mind.
It was as if they pursued me and, having consumed
me, they left me spent, ashen. Tonight, as I sit here,
surrounded by the books that I have written, the
room seems to ring with their permanence, their
rectangular spines like gravestones, yet I hear nothing.*

*And what happened to our own language,
Hannah? Those first glances, the stumbling sentences
that turned to wordless touches. Your hand appearing
in mine as we walked, our footsteps falling in sync.
Half a century of reading each other, of nods and tacit
understanding; of hot stinging words, and midnight
silences in which I lay watching your unsleeping
shape, unable to reach out and touch your shoulder. It
is all slipping from my grasp.*

*It is quiet tonight, in the way that only autumn
can be, and the tawny owls are calling across Berllan-
Deg. I have sat here awhile in the moonlight, feeling
the now rational fear of this cooling body. You will
chastise me tomorrow; I know you will. You will look
at my sullen eyes and say I should rest, but every time
I lay down my head, I am visited by face after face of
people long gone, rising in the darkness.*

*Forgive me, Hannah, for all the ways that I failed
you. I could not have loved you more . . .*

HANNAH WALKED THROUGH THE old trees, her face waxen, her arms aching with work and grief and sleeplessness. She pulled her cardigan around her as the long, dew-silvered grasses dragged at her shoes, the last windfalls slippery underfoot. The house had been full since he died, the old Welsh way of not letting grief sit alone. There had been teacups and saucers to take down from the dresser, chairs to push back against the edges of the parlour. There had been the receiving of neighbours, friends, eager to see her before the funeral so that their private condolences would not have to be given in public. Every morning a slew of new cards, adorned with black crosses, to place on the mantelpiece. Hannah felt the dampness clinging to her skin. No one would call tonight and for that, at least, she was grateful. She felt herself breathe for the first time in a week.

In the end, it had been a protracted farewell. A loss of appetite, and she had tried to cajole him, prepare the foods his mother used to make for him as a child. Sunken cheeks. Eyes. His skin had whitened; his hair seemed almost bleached. She had not been prepared for how beautiful he would look – a shell, an angular form – and she did not leave his side. She took to sleeping in a chair beside him, kissing his cheekbone and touching him semi-awake when he seemed troubled. And at the end, something else she had not been expecting. She had always imagined death as a slipping away, a letting go of life, but it wasn't. Death was more purposeful than that; it was a leaving, a going somewhere else. She had recognized it in the last look in his eyes, the final shudder and the single tear that had rolled down his cheek. He had left her.

Tonight, she had eaten alone, pushed the table up against the wall and placed the food in her mouth though she felt no hunger for it. She had listened, too, to the profound silence. The feet-thick walls of the old house deadened most sound from the outside, and the books which lined them muffled it even more, but the quality of sound was now different. Her knife and fork had clattered on the plate as she suddenly remembered something she ought to have already done. She placed her hands on the table and pushed her weight from the chair, took off her apron and walked up the old cream-painted stairs to the half-landing. There, she opened the linen press and looked at the fabrics folded inside it. She ran her fingers over them for a moment. Some darned in patches by her mother. Blankets and tablecloths from her 'bottom drawer', kept for best and unused; tapestry bedspreads, each one an ache for a past warmth. She found what she wanted and folded it over the crook of her arm.

She had tied his mouth closed with a strip of cloth to stop his jaw gaping, just as she had seen her own mother do when her father died. It had been one of the things she remembered about that time, standing in the doorway watching as her mother, her hands trembling, did her duty. The old firm of undertakers from the village

4

had come to do the rest, had been respectful and kind; a professional ease with the bureaucracy of death.

And now, once more, a man was laid out in the parlour, ready for the service in the morning, his hair combed.

As Hannah walked through the trees, she took in their trunks which glistened in the dampness, their branches thin and painfully bare. They would usually be washed at this time of year, cleansed and put to rest. She would normally do it herself, tie her hair in a scarf and scrub at their skeletal frames, their familiar trunks and limbs, wondering all the while how life could ever return to them. Tonight, they stood sentinel, their branches feeling for a breeze.

She turned a corner, the material heavy on her arm, and looked through the gloaming towards the hives. His hives. There was no movement. The bees would be in their winter cluster now, turning inwards, preserving themselves. Hannah approached them and listened to the silence a moment before unfolding the black silk and laying it gently over them, the silk rasping slightly against the roughness of the wood and gleaming crow-black in the darkness.

She must tell the bees that he had died. That much she knew. She had seen it done but had no eldest son to do it, as was tradition. She rummaged for the old iron door key that she had slipped into her pocket on her way out of the house. It lay cold in her palm, and she felt its weight in her fingers as she placed it at the door of the hive – a sign that their owner had crossed another threshold. She tried to think of something to say, but she could not find the words so she stood a moment, her hands clasped, her cheeks aching from the polite serenity she had feigned for the past week.

There would be so many people tomorrow, just as there had been all this week. She knew the day would pass in the receiving of sympathies she would not remember, the starched whiteness of lilies and the steam on the vestry window as everyone took tea afterwards, but tonight there was nothing. The stillness she had thus far kept at bay seemed to be growing around her, its purity devastating. She turned to look back through the orchard, at the house where he lay, the hives silent behind her, and thought for a moment of the innumerable seasons they had survived here, the falling blossom turning to fruit, the falling fruit rooting and turning to blossom. This winter would be different. She could feel it in the bitter wind, in an unanswered call, and in the impossibility of his silence.

2

Hannah hadn't slept; she had lain awake in the room above the parlour. At dawn, she pulled herself to sitting, pushed back the blanket and let her feet drop to the floor. She walked across the floorboards towards the low window. This morning there was an opaque early mist punctuated only by scarlet-skinned apples among the fallen leaves. For a moment she recalled how she used to sit in her father's lap, listening wide-eyed as he whispered stories of how apples had followed the pilgrims across Europe from east to west, how on a stormy night a ship had been wrecked on the West Wales coast, splitting open barrels of apples which came ashore and rooted themselves along the coastline. Now the orchard remained stubbornly shrouded and she turned and made her way down the stairs, her fingers finding their way along the banister as they had done for well over half a century.

It was dark inside the house this morning, the only light diffusing into the kitchen coming from the warm lamp which she'd left on in the parlour to keep him company. She moved to the stove and made some tea, then carried it over to the table. As she sat, she pressed her palms on to the surface, felt the grain of the wood.

Her father had felled the pear tree, had told her the story a thousand times. How rare it was to find a pear tree with wood straight enough, how old the tree must have been to yield so much to work with. You planted pears for your heirs, their slow growth making their cultivation a small hope for the future. She traced the patterns of the knots, the fingerprint of the orchard. At first when her mother scoured the wood, it had marked, but over time, each blemish had seemed to bleed into another, and the wood had hardened to a deep shine.

She turned her head for a moment, the silence disturbed by the sound of a startled blackbird and some familiar footsteps. She heard them pause at the door and her jaw tightened. She could sense her there, standing on the slate doorstep worn from a thousand comings and goings, wondering whether to knock. She didn't. Hannah kept her eyes on the table as a draught reached her and her sister walked in.

'Hannah?'

Hannah listened as she closed the door behind her, her breathing in disarray after having walked from the road.

'I came as quickly as I could,' she said, her Welsh a little stilted. 'I was away or I would have come sooner.'

Hannah considered her voice. Although her accent had softened from years of living in the city, her voice still contained the same childlike apprehension, a certain defensiveness.

Hannah waited as her sister took her in, suddenly self-conscious at being caught in her nightdress, her hand going to her unbrushed hair.

'Sit. I'll make you some tea,' Hannah said, still not having looked directly at her.

Hannah retreated over the uneven flagstones and waited for the kettle to boil. She stood with her back towards Sadie, feeling the strange, stubborn familiarity of her sister's nearness. Hannah was six years older than Sadie, and today she could feel each one of her seventy years in her body. Was aware, from the fit of her clothes, that her frame had shrunk a little lately. Where Hannah had been tall, fair, Sadie had always been dark-haired and strong.

'Do you still take sugar?' Hannah caught Sadie unawares.

'Yes . . .' Sadie cleared her throat. 'Yes.'

Sadie took the tea, and the sisters sat down. They had not sat together like this for years, and Sadie considered how the house itself seemed outside time, their childhood and their present existing simultaneously here around the table. The kitchen was still as their mother had kept it – plates on racks, a settle on one side of the table, an old television covered with a cloth, and china dogs on the mantelpiece on either side of an old slate clock. Sadie sat watching the steam curling up from their cups, feeling a sudden grief of her own, a pang of emptiness and longing that had something to do with how much Hannah was beginning to look like their mother.

'It's like nothing's changed,' said Sadie quietly.

She regretted her words immediately.

'I mean, in the house, the orchard . . .' she continued.

'Everything's changed,' countered Hannah.

'Of course.' Sadie bowed her head.

'Hannah, I'm sorry,' she said eventually.

'You don't have to say that,' answered Hannah, her eyes flitting away.

'I'm sorry he's gone.' Sadie tried to find Hannah's gaze. 'And I'm sorry I wasn't here to help you.'

'You live too far away; it's to be expected.'

Sadie could feel the curtness in her sister's voice, watched as she picked some down off her nightdress impatiently and flicked it away.

'Who's taking the service?' Sadie asked quietly.

'Evans.'

Sadie nodded.

'There'll be a short service here before . . .'

'He's still here?' exclaimed Sadie, her eyes darting to the half-open door to the parlour. 'I didn't realize . . .'

'Of course he's still here,' chided Hannah.

Sadie felt a stab of guilt at the thought of her sister here alone with him all night.

'The women from the chapel are insisting on making tea in the vestry after the service,' Hannah said.

'He would've liked that.'

'It'll be something for them to do, I suppose,' replied Hannah tartly.

It was getting lighter now, although the winter sun barely illuminated the room. Sadie reached for something to say but her mind seemed to falter.

'I'd better get changed; everyone will be here soon,' Hannah said, standing up abruptly.

Sadie noticed that her tea was untouched.

'I won't be long,' Hannah said before walking to the stairs, leaving Sadie by the table alone.

They shouldered him through the orchard past the shrouded hives, as he had requested. Hannah knew that he was not heavy now, but the ease with which the men with patent shoes carried him was painful; the weight and space he had taken up in her life so seemingly insignificant. Hannah followed on foot towards the hearse, her eyes fixed on the coffin, a white handkerchief pressed into her palm. She found herself turning inwards, barely aware of her sister by her side.

The chapel stood alone next to the road a few miles from Berllan-Deg, its iron gates flaking. It was big enough to accommodate both those invited and those whose relationship with Hannah's husband had been more casual, to sit in the gallery above. Hannah always thought that Welsh funerals were cruel: their public nature, the way some villagers relished attending each one, however casual the acquaintance. The parading of grief. Sadie used always to insist that grief was collective; it could not be extricated or kept to yourself. It was no good trying to control it to suit your own convenience.

Today the winter light streamed in through the jewelled tones of the windows, the over-painted walls growing damp from the heat of the congregation. Hannah followed the coffin inside, keeping her eyes on the trembling flowers on its lid as it was moved. She could hear the muffled hymns as if through her body more than her mind, the collective breaths, the subdued pedal organ. There were Welsh hymns from their childhood; some unfamiliar English ones, too, which she had trusted the minister to choose, as there were staff here from the library, and some from his days at the university. She was sure the eulogies were respectful, but she struggled to comprehend the words as they dissipated into the cavernous space.

Her mind turned to the day they married, how they had stood here in the same place under the pulpit. The thin dress she had worn, his dark-blue suit a little too big. The trembling deep down inside her, the cold, the nervousness. The way he hadn't shaved as he had been up all night, the neighbourhood boys firing shots into the dark, felling trees on to the road, trying to stop him arriving at the chapel. The way the village children had placed a rope across the road, so she had to pay to pass. A performance, rituals representing the obstacles that they would have to endure. She remembered the lunch they had had in the hotel in the village, and how he had held court during the speeches, the muffled laughter.

Now the last hymn had been sung and Hannah became aware once again of the silence. The minister invited everyone to the vestry afterwards for refreshments, and then it was time, time to follow him once more down the aisle. The cold air made her gasp as she emerged behind him. There was a short service by the graveside, a few more prayers, and then the mourners filed past her with damp handshakes and whispered condolences, until she was left alone with Sadie. The gravediggers in their mud-covered denim were smoking on the other side of the chapel out of respect. Hannah turned back towards the grave one last time before walking the thin path to the vestry.

The chapel women were in their element; aprons over black blouses, they bustled around the serving hatch, pouring tea from aluminium teapots polished like pennies. Groups of men put the world to rights, their ties slackened a little by now. Hannah sat with Sadie, but she could not find a place for her grief among the thinly sliced brown bread, the caraway cake and the laughter. She drank some tea, then slipped the envelope containing what she owed the chapel for the provisions to Sadie, to pass on discreetly.

It was getting late when they arrived home. Hannah closed the door behind her and began to clear the morning's teacups. One of them slid on its saucer, rattling loudly, and Hannah suddenly seemed unsteady. Sadie reached out and held her arm tightly as Hannah righted herself. They stood for a moment in stillness.

'I'm all right,' she said eventually, shaking off Sadie's hand.

'Sit down. I'll do that,' answered Sadie, taking the cup from her hand. She tried not to look as Hannah took a seat, her face pale against the harsh darkness of her blouse.

'I'll stay for a week or two,' Sadie said as she filled the old sink to wash the dishes.

Hannah didn't reply.

'If that's all right?'

Afterwards, Sadie made more tea, stirred some sugar into it, and they sat once again in silence. As darkness fell, Hannah looked over at the parlour. The door had been left open, the furniture still pushed back. An empty space at the heart of the house.

3

HANNAH WASN'T EATING OR sleeping properly. Sadie had been watching her for the past few days; she had done nothing but pace around the house tidying away John's possessions, and if she rested at all, her unease would be evident in the way she would sit on the edge of the seat as if ready to get up at any moment. Sadie could hear her upstairs making a start on sorting his clothes, pulling them from the old wardrobe and packing them into boxes. This was what Hannah would do; when anything significant happened to her, she would disappear into herself, revert to doing the right thing, doing her duty, as best she could.

Sadie found herself on her own in the house for long periods of time and felt both strangely at home and completely disorientated. She did not think she had ever felt as if she had fully inhabited the place. As a child, her stations around the house had been confined to its edges. She would sit on the landing, where she would overhear hushed conversations, or hide on the wide window seats, where she would often draw the curtains and observe life through the crack. The vast age difference between her and Hannah had for the most part characterized their relationship, their interests, their understanding, but there had also been a few golden years when they had come together; those early teenage years when Hannah had been afraid enough of her own burgeoning body to humour her young sister and retreat into the freedom of childhood. For one glorious summer or two, the orchard had sung with magic and infinite possibilities.

Hannah had always felt more at home in the orchard; it was as if you could not tell where the orchard ended and Hannah began. In those days they would climb trees, eat apples until they were sick. Hannah would hang a rope from tree to tree and fold an old bedsheet over it, take a lamp inside and act out shadowy plays until Sadie cried with laughter. She would imitate the adults who came to visit – their mannerisms, their speech – and tell Sadie to do the same because she knew that, being younger, her sister would not get into trouble in the same way she would. In the autumn, they would light fires under the peerless skies, talk about how Hannah was destined to become an actress and how Sadie would be a journalist, that she would have her own newspaper and write about the films her sister was in. But as Hannah grew into a young woman, their mother had started to chide her for being too loud, and some of the village boys would sit on the old stone bridge and shout things at her blossoming beauty as she walked home from school. Hannah would stay in her room more, leaving Sadie to play alone. Sadie only loved the orchard if Hannah was there, and by the time Sadie grew into herself, Berllan-Deg had begun to feel claustrophobic, lonely.

She had not come to see Hannah and John often after she left Berllan-Deg, but the house certainly felt different without his presence. Sadie opened the curtains and looked out at the spot where she had first seen him. She had sat on the wide windowsill overlooking the front door, watching as he picked up her sister. He had looked old to Sadie's ten-year-old eyes, even though, of course, he wasn't. An innate confidence, an ease about him that Sadie had spent years trying to develop and knew she still didn't possess. She had listened to their hushed greeting, Hannah throwing her coat over her thin shoulders, his hand going to her waist as they walked away, and then his head turning, catching Sadie's eye. He had winked at her, making Sadie pull back from the window, her face flushing with an irritation that would endure. It wasn't as if he was ever unpleasant to her; quite the opposite, in fact. He had bought her sweets and magazines, and had humoured her when she'd asked provocatively whether all the girls were so easily impressed, so easily bought. It was more the way he had taken it for granted that Hannah would marry him, and her sister's infuriating acquiescence, that had irked her.

After the funeral, Hannah had asked her to start going through his paperwork. The door of his office stood open, his glasses on the table as if he had just left. Sadie's ambition of becoming a journalist had been short-lived, and she had become a teacher. It was something she could politely speak to John about on the rare occasions she and Seth had visited. She walked towards the office and moved inside. His desk was characteristically neat, the chair pushed back slightly, a saggy threadbare velvet cushion which had probably once been for best, a pen on the floor. She would need to find his documents, his accounts; at least she could do that for Hannah.

When Sadie was older, she would sit on the bed, watching as Hannah got ready for dances in the town hall. John would come and fetch her and then Sadie would lie awake, waiting for the headlights to light up the orchard when Hannah arrived home. Sadie would creep to the window and look out as they bade each other goodnight, her heart beating faster at the excitement of it all, before jumping back into bed when she heard her sister's footsteps on the stairs. Hannah would brush out her hair, get into bed next to her, know that Sadie had crept out of bed from the coolness of her skin. When Sadie couldn't contain herself any longer, she would start to question Hannah relentlessly in the dark about who she'd seen, what music had been played, while Hannah shushed her, saying she had a headache.

Sadie had already guessed that something was wrong. John's mother was incandescent, apparently, what with him going off to university. Their own mother wouldn't even look at Hannah. Then, desperate, Hannah had asked Sadie to go fetch John, to bring him to Berllan-Deg, and Sadie had snuck out of the house through the orchard. By the time they returned, it was too late. Hannah had been taken to town. Sadie waited in her bedroom, her knees tucked under her chin, until they came back, and then she could do nothing but keep her company as Hannah lay curled up. And then came the bleeding, the relentless bleeding that made even their mother blanch, and then the fever and the infection, the fluttering pulse and eventually the hospital when the need for treatment had overridden the knowledge that once the local nurses knew, everybody would know. Sadie had spent the months afterwards reading to Hannah while Hannah stared out at the autumning orchard.

By the time Hannah was well enough to come downstairs, she was absent from herself, indifferent. John had visited her before he went to university. Sadie remembered it well. Their father had stayed in the orchard chopping wood and their mother had made some tea, but only tea, no bread and butter. He was given the sparsest of welcomes and Sadie had gone outside to the rear of the house and stood with her back to the wall next to the parlour window while they sat and talked.

John had left to study languages, like his mother wanted him to, but he came home every summer. His life seemed untouched, while Hannah was treated as sullied by their mother and those at the chapel. The whispers were loud.

What infuriated Sadie more than anything was that once John had finished his university course, he came home and they married anyway. Sadie was stuffed into a high-collared dress, their mother still not looking entirely pleased. This was not the way things were supposed to go, their mother would reiterate to Hannah frequently. After a brief honeymoon on the coast, the couple had moved in with Sadie and her parents and they had lived a tense existence together until Sadie had managed to leave.

Sadie listened now, as she heard footsteps descending the staircase, heard Hannah scraping the fireplace in the kitchen. Through the open office door, she saw her walk out of the front door with a pail in her hand.

Sadie followed her out and watched as Hannah walked in circles around a few of the trees, tipping the ashes on to the orchard floor. An old habit that did the trees good, a kind of giving back. Hannah would not place the ashes at the base of the trees, but out in a circle where the branches ended, as she knew that the roots extended that far. It was still today, the wind not disturbing the ashes as she walked. Sadie thought back to the time when a tree had blown over in strong winds and she and Hannah had gone to look at its roots, upturned and obscene somehow. Sadie had thought then that a tree was two trees, really, two lives – one you could see, and one you could not.

Hannah straightened up and walked back towards the house.

'It feels like so long ago, doesn't it?'

Hannah looked at her.

'When we were children . . . I was listening to the minister at the funeral,' said Sadie, 'talking about the Garden of Eden.'

Hannah didn't move but glanced up towards the darkening sky.

'It wasn't a garden, though, was it?' she continued. 'It was an orchard.'

4

GRIEF WAS A LESSON that Hannah would have to learn and relearn a hundred times a day. For although she knew the fact of John's death, she did not know the reality of it. She had found that her mind would be drawn into something sometimes, and she would look across the kitchen and think that she needed to wash his coat, only to remember that he was gone. She would lay a hand over on his side of the bed in the dark of the night and find her palm flat on the mattress and remember that he was gone. She would think that she had something to tell him, something even about his own death, and remember that he was gone. She would shake her head at the absurdity of it and try to quell the sickness that would surge through her stomach. It seemed that his death would rain down on her in a thousand slow drips of understanding.

Yesterday, she had folded his clothes away, the suits he kept for best, checking their pockets to find handkerchiefs and invitations to functions that they had been to years ago. A tie shoved into a pocket, having been loosened after the stuffy part of the evening and eventually tugged off completely on the way home. The V-neck jumpers he wore at home because he could not stand a high collar; the old tweed jackets that sagged at the elbows. She had pressed them all into boxes, the memories rising around her, trying not to think, trying not to lose herself.

Today she had begun on his bedside cabinet: the spare reading glasses, the books, the tablets and the clock. When he had first moved in, he had only brought a few clothes. Her mother had reiterated that things were to be left as they were, and it was made clear to them that there was no space for any new furniture or furnishings. Hannah had put the linens and blankets they had received on their wedding in the linen press, and they had stayed there. She and John had had to make themselves small; John's token income from the university was pitiful and the cost of travelling there and back every day significant. Hannah had worked for a year at a local office, typing, but when they married, she had to stop working, as was expected. John would contribute to the bills, of course, and help her father at the weekends. At first John had found humour in the situation, would tease her mother by using the wrong cup, or by making a show of not putting his chair back under the table as he was meant to and winking at Hannah. He would read out loud sometimes, risqué passages from books which made her father study his own book with more intensity, and her mother boil with indignation. Then, as the supposedly temporary situation continued, things became more strained. His income fell further when he began writing more, and after years of marriage there were still no children. By the time Sadie left, their mother had stopped pretending to have forbearance and John would go outside and tend to his bees.

It was only after her father died and her mother became ill, and was increasingly confined to one room, that the house had gradually become theirs. Hannah had gone to town and chosen some of her own tableware, and John had bought himself a cushion and a chair. The strange thing was that by then they had grown into their inherited nest, so much so that they did not have a new vision for it, as they might have done when they were younger.

Hannah pressed a hand on the bed and pushed herself up. She stood on his side of the bed for a moment, looking at the empty wardrobe in front of her, the doors still open. She gripped the bag containing his things, an ache in her chest which sharpened at each remembrance.

Later that morning, Hannah took the vase down from the mantelpiece. The white flowers had yellowed and discoloured, so she threw them into the fire, listened to the crackle. She folded the sympathy cards one after another and placed them in the dresser drawer. She had stripped all the beds and put the second load of washing on. She could hear Sadie sifting quietly through papers in the office, her movements around the house becoming more familiar.

Hannah had looked after Sadie when she was brought home from the hospital as a baby, as their mother had been ill and the doctor had told her to lie on her front for weeks on end to help her stomach retract. Hannah had woken at night to give her milk, and after that the child would only take milk from Hannah. Her father always used to say how good she was with her, what a natural mother she was. What her father didn't know was that Hannah hated Sadie for a long time. The way everyone looked past her and at Sadie whenever they came to the house, how boring it was to play with a sister so much younger. She resented the way she'd be left with Sadie while her parents went to the village, and sometimes she'd hit back when Sadie hit her, even though she was much older and should have known better.

Looking after Sadie had been too much for her as a young girl and, as the years progressed, she swore she would never have a child herself. Not for a long time, anyway. Her only escape was the town library, which her mother allowed her to visit on Saturday mornings when she was shopping in town. Hannah used to impress upon her how she could never keep Sadie quiet there and that she would have to go alone. Picking out some books for Sadie was a small price to pay. That was where, at sixteen, she had seen John for the first time and felt a jolt of something.

Hannah looked towards the window now; it was a bright winter's day but the light inside was dull. She boiled the kettle on the stove and poured the water into a bowl, then rummaged under the sink for the rags she had made from an old bedsheet. The windows were covered in a grey film of dust and ash from the fire, and she had not cleaned them for months. She worked her way around the four panes inside, rinsing the cloth every now and again, and baulked as the grime gave way under the scalding water. Even before she'd begun on the outside, she could see that the quality of light in the kitchen had changed.

The windows at the back of the house were smaller, to keep the warmth in. The parlour had always been her mother's pride and joy, away from the dust and mud, the comings and goings of the kitchen. A place where she could be confident she could welcome visitors at any time, although they rarely had any. Hannah remembered her father wondering out loud about the logic of keeping the best room in the house clean for people who never came. When Hannah and John had married, she had asked her mother if they could have it as a sitting room, somewhere they could go for some privacy, but her mother had refused and, even after her parents' death, Hannah and John had got used to not using it unless in exceptional circumstances. It had become a room set apart from living, a strange ideal that allowed you to sit outside your life for a moment.

Hannah cleaned the last window, threw away the dirty water and walked to the tap at the side of the house to wash out the bowl before leaving it on the floor to dry. She wiped her hands on her corduroy trousers and opened the door to find Sadie standing at the table, letters spread out in front of her. The look in her eyes made Hannah's heart leap.

'What is it?' she asked. 'What's happened?'

Hannah noticed Sadie's hands were trembling.

5

HANNAH SAT UNCOMPREHENDING; HER sister had just read the will to her, but she still couldn't understand. It was as if the words had passed her by or were in another language.

'There must be some mistake,' she said, her voice dangerously clipped.

Sadie had read the whole thing twice.

'There's no mistake,' Sadie answered softly.

Hannah got up abruptly and walked towards the sink. She began to clear the breakfast dishes but, as she did so, she saw that her own hands were shaking.

'Hannah, he has a daughter.'

The cups slipped from her hands, clattered into the sink. The words seemed to fill the kitchen, suffocating them both.

'Who is she?' Hannah asked.

'It says her name is Megan. There's not much else, apart from her birth date,' Sadie said, trying to keep her voice small.

Hannah hadn't noticed at first, but she had cut her hand and it was bleeding on to the ceramic sink. She watched as her blood swirled into the water.

'He's left you some letters, too,' Sadie persisted.

Hannah turned and Sadie was momentarily frightened by her appearance.

'I don't want them.'

Sadie looked down at the eleven letters enfolded

in the will, began to spread them out on the table.

'But they might explain . . .'

'I said I don't want them!'

There was a terrible stillness to Hannah now, her hands behind her, her knuckles whitening under the grip she had on the kitchen unit.

'Did you know?' she asked her sister, bullet-like.

Sadie shook her head. 'No.'

'But you're vindicated now, aren't you? The way you felt about him.' She strung out the words. 'What else does the will say? Let me see it.'

'I just read it to you . . .'

'I said let me see!'

Sadie was startled by the tone of her voice. Hannah walked towards her and snatched the document, tried to read it but the words danced on the page. She stood, trying to comprehend. He had a daughter. She threw down the letter, wet and smudged with her blood, her hands trembling with a rage she could not contain, then abruptly headed towards his office. She spotted the box Sadie had been sorting through and she pulled at it, spilling his papers on to the floor, her arms flailing.

'Hannah!' Sadie cried out, though Hannah could not hear her.

Hannah clawed at the bookshelves, at the neat books in rows, everything ordered, everything immaculate. She could see what she was doing but could not make sense of it: the books falling to the floor, their covers agape, the mess of words.

'Hannah, please.'

Sadie tried to put her hand on her sister's shoulder,

but Hannah pushed her away, walked out over the books, her face ashen.

Hannah made a path towards the hives. It was as if she had left her body, her breath stolen from it. She walked through the grass, a cacophony of noise humming in her head, and when she reached the hives, she pulled at the black silk, yanked it until it tore. She picked up the key and threw it at the wood sharply. It bounced away with a clink. She tried to speak, but couldn't; she tried to scream, but there was nothing. Sadie watched from afar, her hands by her sides, helpless.

And it was then that Hannah felt herself collapsing in on herself, and the agonized sound of her grief brought her sister running. Sadie caught her as Hannah's knees gave way. Sadie listened, terrified, to her wailing, the sound electric around them. It was a deep grief, decades old. The kind of grief that is rarely released. Sadie felt it reverberate from her sister's body into hers and back again, too much for one body to contain. Sadie did not shush Hannah; she would not want to deny her this. She simply held her and rocked her back and forth on the grass, the tense hum of the disturbed hive behind them.

6

*. . . Forgive me, Hannah, for all the ways that I failed
you. I could not have loved you more. I don't know
if I ever told you, Hannah, but the first beehive I had
was shaped like a book, its spine perpendicular to the
floor. My father taught me their language, how to leaf
through the glass-framed leaves and read the signs
left there by the bees. The way they stored memories
of spring hawthorns and hazel coppices, their innate
knowledge of pollen flows and stormy weather.*

*I have long since lost the ability to see those
delicate porcelain-coloured eggs laid by the queen,
and the pearlescent sheen of the larvae. Even the
subtle ochre and warm golds of the pollens are gone
from me now, but I have realized that sight was
only one way to commune with the bees. As my eyes
worsened, I relied more on their vibration underneath
my fingers, their sound, and I suddenly realized how
blind I had been all along. I am glad, though, that
I did not know the last time I would open a hive, to
have that joy remain unadulterated, and I am sorry to
have sulked when you eventually insisted on handing
over their care to Jack.*

*It is as dark as the night gets now, and the tawny
owls have quietened into hunting. I can feel them
knifing the air, their wingtips upturned, looking for
prey. My skin prickles with the thought of them. I
know how tired you are, I know the burden I am*

becoming, and I know you have caught me looking at you, trying to etch your face in my memory. I think of you reading these letters; I think of your face, your heart. I do not know, Hannah, why the world gives us so much only to take it away, why it gives us so many languages just to leave us wordless. Perhaps, it leaves us with only what is important, so I must reach in the dark for those luminous things. The glimmer of honey in the depths of the honeycomb, and the life we made together. I will try to order my thoughts using the only language I have left, and I pray that it will be enough for you.

7

SADIE FILLED A BOWL with water and found a flannel. She placed everything on a tray and carried
it up the creaking stairway. She opened the door, her
heart sinking to see Hannah still sleeping. She opened
the curtains, trying to get as much light into the room
as winter allowed. Hannah had slept for days, and
Sadie was afraid she might disappear completely if she
didn't stir a little. She set the tray down on the wide
windowsill, wetted the flannel, and made her way over
to the bed.

She washed Hannah's hands first, gently. Watched
as her wedding ring momentarily steamed under the
heat of the cloth. The ring was worn thin with age and
work. Then she washed her forearms and dried them
with a towel. She saw her sister's eyelids flickering.
She washed her face next, wondering where the face she
knew had gone. Hannah had never seen it herself, but
there was a great beauty about her. The strange thing
was that she had always been a bystander to it, as though
the world had given it to her, but it didn't belong to her.
Her face had changed, of course – dark spots clustering
around her eyes, the thinning of her lips – but it was
more than that, too. It was as if the world had pushed
her out of herself, made her stand beside herself and
find herself lacking.

Hannah opened her eyes and held Sadie's hand
silently.

'It's been days,' Sadie said gently. 'You've not eaten . . .'

Her sister looked exhausted, frail almost. It had rained incessantly through the night, rivulets sweeping through the orchard and washing away the dregs of the last leaves. Hannah looked past her towards the window and Sadie followed her gaze; then, not sure what to say next, she pulled at the corner of the cover and got into the bed next to Hannah. Hannah felt her warmth, a physical memory stirring somewhere of the two of them under the covers.

'How could he have left me with this?' Hannah asked simply. 'All the years we had, all the months and years and decades. He had so much time. How can you grieve for someone you don't know?'

'He loved you, Hannah. This news doesn't change that.'

'I didn't know him. He was my whole life . . . my one life . . . and . . .' Her words gaped, were cavernous.

Sadie reached for her hand.

'If there's one thing I've learnt these past few years, it's that we can be so vast . . . all of us, we can hold so many things.'

'Don't make excuses for him.'

Sadie did not know what to say, wanted to offer some comfort but knew that there was little to give.

'I've been going over and over things,' Hannah said eventually. 'If the girl is in her twenties now, he must have been almost fifty when she was born, Sadie.' There was a horror in her eyes now. 'He wasn't young, or stupid.'

'Why don't you read the letters?'

Hannah began shaking her head.

'No, I can barely . . . I can't think of him whispering in my ear like that.'

Sadie squeezed her hand again.

'The thing is that I'm too old, too old to be jealous or lovesick.'

'Don't say that,' replied Sadie.

'Do you think people knew?' Hannah searched Sadie's face.

'I don't think so.'

Outside, the rain was gathering in the guttering, falling chaotically across the window. They sat in silence for a moment.

'The strangest thing is to think that part of him lives on, in this woman. Sadie . . .' Hannah looked her in the eye. 'I think I need to meet her. I want you to bring her here.'

Sadie stared at her in shock, shook her head, her whole body revolting against the idea. 'I don't think that's a—'

'Sadie, please? Ask her to come?'

'But Hannah, why? What could you gain from that?' She looked at Hannah in confusion.

'I need to see her, with my own eyes.'

There was an earnestness there now, a desperation that Sadie had not seen before.

'I need to see her,' Hannah repeated. 'Do this for me.'

8

Hive

The nest is built in the centre of the hive in the shape of a sphere. A globe hung through eleven frames; a world suspended. By opening a hive this way, you can dissect the nest slice by slice and inspect it. It is at once a complete orb, and several separate cross sections, all eleven of them. The frames at the sides are usually quieter, emptier, the bees having pulled out the honeycomb a little, perhaps; then, as you get nearer the heart, towards the frames where the queen usually resides, it is busier. There is language, and brood, pollen and eggs; there are signs that can easily be read and symbols that I do not think we will ever understand. Then, as we work our way towards the edge once more, things quieten again. The opening of a hive is a journey, you could say, to the heart of the hive and out again, a loving assessment of the world they have built.

If I am given enough time, I will write you eleven letters, Hannah, if you'll read them?

You know, I've noticed that the shape of a hive is only important to people. Left to their own devices, bees will build their comb in swags, curved and theatrical. Although their cells have a certain rigidity of shape, the bees choose in general to build in undulations; straight lines don't seem to please them. To be truthful, I think they would always prefer trees to nest in. They are drawn to old ones, ones whose heartwood has loosened a little. I imagine them enjoying their own vibrations, humming within the hollowed-out trunks. I have seen skeps, too, made of straw, in which they build looser forms, but now we insist on cedar for man's convenience, so we can take what we want with ease. We have made the bees live in houses. A roof, a place to store honey, a nest, a floor, a door, and even though they acquiesce, they still rebel. They will seal out draughts with sticky propolis; they will build between the frames, their creativity spilling over. For the queen cells, they construct golden pot-bellied chalices at the edges of the comb so that she emerges, like a child, upside down. After her birth, she rests before her maiden flight and the beginning of a life of labour.

I am sorry that we had to make our life with your parents at Berllan-Deg. I am sorry that I didn't earn enough to find our own house. I saw the way you struggled to be both eldest daughter and new wife. They say you should never place a hive under trees, for fear of the rain collecting in the leaves above and the constant drip on to the hives driving the bees to distraction. I heard the relentlessness of your mother's words, her stinging remarks. The way she would rewash the clothes after you had laundered them, the way she would lay the table for four instead of five, and the way you would wordlessly fetch me a plate and cutlery and lay them on the table next to yours.

But at least we had a place to store some honey, somewhere to carry our worries. That new bed. The

34

*anticipation, the possibilities, the trying to be quiet.
Your curls undone and the slip of that satin strap off
your shoulder. The way we tried to wrestle a new
language for ourselves, a belief that we would escape
and a hope that things would change. We had a roof
and some room for sweetness, but we did not have our
nest. That would have to wait.*

*I don't know why we force the bees into hives; it
is almost as if we convince ourselves that it has always
been this way. It is easier for us, so that is what we do,
and we do not consider what the bees need or how a
new queen begins her days. The way she is specifically
fed, manipulated and prepared for her life, the
way she has no alternative. How young she is, how
blinkered, as she emerges blissfully unaware of the
weight of expectation already on her shoulders.*

*Despite standing alone, a hive cannot exist in
isolation. Although set apart, perhaps, in an orchard,
a quiet place, it is in fact part of the fabric of its
surroundings. It is an indicator of its environment's
health. Its success depends on a thousand subtle
things, some of which it can control, some it cannot. I
have heard a hive pulsate with a million wings as the
workers fan down the heat of summer; I have found
a hive starved to death after a farmer decided that this
was the year to plough all the flowers back into the
field. Some years are overrun with honey, in others
the bees' survival hangs by a thread.*

*Perhaps it was because we could not really
inhabit the house that I began the apiary at Berllan-
Deg. It allowed me to excuse myself when it suited*

me, stake a claim, make my presence felt in a way that did not challenge your father. The bees served the trees and vice versa. I knew he measured a man by his actions, and I knew how mistrustful he was of men who used language loosely.

When your father died, I helped carry him from Berllan-Deg and watched as you winced under your mother's worsening sharpness. I saw you tend to her, while I retreated more and more to the apiary. I saw your dismay when her loss of memory began to reveal a depth of unselfconscious cruelty that you could not even have imagined was there, and I noticed the way you masked your relief when she died. I know you were relieved, Hannah, and just a part of you will be relieved when I die, because you are human, because you are tired, because waiting for the inevitable is exhausting.

I have concluded that those hives shaped like books were cruel. Their frames seemed too narrow, the sheets of honeycomb contained in glass almost voyeuristic now, their leaves unable to contain the enormity of what was being written there. Those panes were crude, made by someone who thought they could frame nature herself. As crude as an attempt to learn more about a butterfly by slicing a pin through its thorax. Much like my books. My dictionary, my collection of words in a language only spoken by a few. Each word dissected and defined, pulled apart as it yearned for life, for what use are words if they lie dead on the page? Each word an approximation that falls so short of what we experience that recently I have brought myself to silence.

36

I was never content with my first hives, which is why I settled eventually on ones made from wood harvested around Berllan-Deg. A simple structure placed where the sun touches first in midwinter. A few moments of extra warmth in the early spring can mean the difference between life and death. I raised them up a little from the floor, and in winter would take blankets and place them underneath the roof. I tried to protect them from the harshest weather, and I tried to do the same for you. I tried to shield you from the worst cold, and perhaps that was my greatest mistake.

9

THE BOOKS LAY ON the floor of John's office like broken birds, their pages splayed across the tiles, their spines twisted. Sadie began scooping them up and stacking them haphazardly back on the shelves, not caring whether John would begrudge her the lack of order or not. She gathered the ones that he had written himself and put those in the desk drawer. Hannah had eventually come out of her bed, but had been quiet these past few days, unable to settle anywhere, a palpable restlessness in her that agitated each room whenever she entered and made Sadie wonder whether sending the letter to Megan was sensible. She had ventured to question Hannah again this morning, asked her if she had considered whether the girl would even come, and how that might make her feel, but her sister had been adamant.

Sadie had never felt responsible for Hannah; their relationship had always been one-sided like that. She had felt dependent on her, yes, had felt her own decisions were silently judged, but since returning home and seeing her sister's distress she had begun to feel something else. The strange separation that came from caring for Hannah. She felt the weight of the pen in her hand as she tried to put down the difficult words, the news of his death, not knowing how they would be received. She had never been a writer, not in the way John had been. There was an ease in his grasp of language that she would never have, a knack of order-ing words so that they were at their strongest and had exactly the right effect. She had always been more prac-tical, would have to practise what she wanted to say. She sat for what seemed like hours before settling on one draft that was slightly more coherent than the others, the language neutral, matter-of-fact. She folded the paper and pushed it into an envelope before writing a covering letter to the solicitor.

Her own life had been inundated by such missives over the past few years, as tearful conversations with her husband had turned into silence, distance, then let-ters sent by other people. The coldness of the tone, the descriptive language aimed at creating hurt to generate income for the middleman. Each letter an onslaught, a bruise, so much so that she had sickened at every arrival, until they had stopped, and the final silence started. She looked now for the solicitor's address and scrawled it on the envelope, pressed enough stamps on it, and then decided to walk to the postbox on the lane before she changed her mind.

Hannah had tried to rest, had tried to lie on the bed, but was too exhausted to sleep and – despite Sadie's presence in the office – she felt an exquisite loneliness that noth-ing seemed to relieve. She had walked downstairs and paced the kitchen for a while before going to the dresser and opening the drawers, pulling out albums, pictures, one after another. Images of another time. Her father, her mother, sitting at the seaside; her mother with her skirt hitched up to her knees, relaxing in a deckchair, her father shielding his eyes from the sun. John and her, sitting on the bonnet of his first car; his oiled hair, her floral dress. Her as carnival queen, a cloak around her and a diamanté tiara on her head. There was a wedding album, too, cards she had kept. Letters and telegrams sent to the hotel where they had had their wedding breakfast. Some love spoons she had been given that day still on their mottled and faded ribbons.

She had lived a life with him, she thought as she looked at the images; this was her evidence. The pictures told her that she was not going mad, that their life together had been real. She had married him, and they had had a good life together and nothing could change that. Surely nothing could change that? He had held her when she was grieving the loss of yet another baby; he had squeezed her hand at her mother's funeral; he used to take her for fish and chips on a Sunday evening and they would sit next to the window, their mugs of tea steaming; she had stood next to him proudly at the launch of his dictionary, and other books, at the library. She had stood waiting while he chatted to people, as he signed books, and he had looked over at her, caught her eye and smiled. The plastic medical beakers she had helped him drink from at the end of his life were still here, the stick that he had used to walk still leant against the doorframe; everything about him was familiar, yet he had a daughter.

Hannah felt the weight of those words anew. Her grief was shattering, shattered, displaced. She did not know what she was grieving for. Was it him, the idea of him, the idea of the life they'd had together? Or was it the jealousy and shame and contempt and anger filling her up, growing inside her so she felt that at any moment she might be torn apart?

'Hannah?' It was Sadie, her cheeks cold from walking along the lane. She pulled off her coat, hung it on a peg, and came towards her.

'Hannah, what are you doing?'

Hannah shook her head. Sadie tried not to step on some of the photographs that had spilled on to the floor. She bent to pick them up, placed them back on the table.

Hannah was scaring her.

'Hannah, say something?'

She was still shaking her head.

Sadie tried to find her eyes with her own.

'Hannah, please say something. You've got to put this grief somewhere' – Sadie's voice was breaking now – 'or it will kill you. Believe me, it will kill you, Hannah.'

Sadie held her, felt her sister's body rigid and unyielding in her arms.

Hannah was trying to articulate something, but she was guttural, voiceless. Sadie pulled Hannah towards her and, slowly, Hannah's body began to soften a little.

'Come on,' Sadie whispered. 'Come on.'

She felt the tears on her face as Hannah rested her head as lightly as a bird on her shoulder.

10

Queen

There is a common misconception about the queen,
that she is somehow a spoilt dictator languishing on
the comb, being waited upon hand and foot, when in
fact she is the hive's servant. Its creative force, if you
will. The queen is captive and is only allowed to leave
the hive once, on her wedding day; after that, her life is
dedicated to those around her and she must live selflessly.

The most remarkable thing is that she is born
from an egg like any other, but she is chosen, fed
something that changes her before she has a mind of
her own. Nourished so that she turns into a queen
who will live for two years or more, which for a bee
must seem like an eternity. Days before her release
from her cell, she begins to scream with anguish – I
have heard it myself, Hannah. A mixture of rage,
indignation and frustration, and when she is released,
she is driven by only one desire, and that is to kill her
mother. It seems her creativity can only begin once she
has eliminated every other version of tomorrow.

I heard you, Hannah. I begged my mother, my
father, to let us marry but I was cut off, shut out. I
was young and I know that isn't an excuse, but it
didn't cross my mind to disobey them, to take things
into my own hands.

When the queen leaves the hive to find her mate,
the whole colony takes up a minor-key hum. Their

*future hangs on her success, so she flies upwards,
upwards, calling on all potential mates, and as she
flies higher, only the strongest, most worthy suitors
prevail. Having tested her own strength, she is left
with the only suitor that matches her spirit. She
returns to take her place and the future of the hive
is secure.*

*I did not match you, Hannah, I watched you
go. I trusted that they knew what they were doing;
I trusted my elders. I trusted that you would be well
looked after and that things could be repaired; I
trusted in how things worked.*

*I have often thought how cruel the deception
is. The young queen returned, hailed as architect,
author. The way all the bees dance to greet her, the
ease with which she lays her first eggs, dropping them
in curves. Commas in hexagons. Two thousand a
day, her body aching with potential, and then, one
day, it becomes more difficult, and the whispering
starts. Signals carried from one bee to another; her
fertility, her creativity called into doubt; her sense
of being trapped in a life of giving. If she is found
lacking, a rumour begins to spread which makes her
work harder; the growing sense of unrest, of criticism,
encircles her, fills her with a depth of dread.*

*That first miscarriage felt like the cruellest; the
fact that there was no warning, no bleeding. A quiet
miscarriage and a life stalled. The hush of the nurse as
she listened for a heartbeat that had long since stilled,
the weeks the child took to come away and then the
silence. What scared me most was the way your open*

face changed. Your smile became more conscious and, as the months rolled on, the questions began, casual, invasive. When would the baby come? The way you breezily brushed them away, the way you began to hold people at arm's length. Polite but cold. You would come to bed and turn your back to me; I think you saw yourself as broken, as somehow deficient. Our promise when we married to make a new start, to begin from the beginning, becoming impossible.

I have seen the brutality of the hive. The way the doubt builds into scorn, the indifference of a community that no longer finds a woman useful, the lack of empathy, the shocking ease with which their regard cools and the way the queen is dragged to the executioner's block. She is killed by a hundred stings so that no one individual feels the need to take responsibility, but even before this, the hive has already begun to cultivate her replacement to their liking. Pliable, eager to please, wanting to create for them. Her first act is to ask for food with humility. The respect shown to the previous queen is transferred to her, for the love and reverence they have for their queen is for 'a queen', not 'the queen'. She is an idea, a symbol, a precarious ideal that seems to hold them all together.

11

WHEN HANNAH WOKE AT dawn, Sadie was still fast asleep. The previous night, her sister had lain on the covers and kept her silent company until both of them had drifted off into an uncomfortable sleep. Hannah listened to Sadie's breathing for a while, looking out at the trees in the orchard. She had a vague recollection that she had dreamt of them, the way they seemed to gather the world around them; she thought about their presence in her life and the way she had always looked out at the world through them. She got up and dressed quietly.

Hannah pulled her coat from the peg and walked out into the morning. The dawn chorus was subdued, the birds still fragile, their lives precarious; their full-throated song would come only with confidence, with the knowledge that the last frosts had passed and that their hopes for summer were relatively secure. There were a few jackdaws arguing this morning, falling chaotically through the sky, a few blue tits questioning. There was a certain delicacy about the orchard, grey-blue and velvety, and she could feel its company around her.

When she was a girl, before Sadie's birth, the trees were her playthings. Things she begged her father to hang ropes from so she could swing. She would clamber over branches, tie twine around them and pretend to ride them like horses, her father's shouts melting into laughter. In summer, the orchard would be resplendent with dozens of varieties of mostly cider apples. Some tiger-striped, some sharp and green and domed, most of them sour. During the day Hannah would spend her time sitting under the trees reading, but then would come the seriousness of the harvest. Rolled-up sleeves and swearing, food brought out into the orchard at night to save time. The blue smoke of the men as they shared cigarettes; the first touches of autumn perceptible in the cooling air. She could almost hear them now, swear that if she turned her head, they'd emerge from the greyness.

Her father would move around the orchard making a distinctive pattern of sounds. Perhaps that's why it had been difficult when she came home from the hospital after the abortion. She had lain in bed thinking he would come to her. She would listen, listen, know where he was at any given time. She would hear the shed door close, would hear the axe, but she did not hear his footsteps on the landing leading to her door. At first, she had thought that he was just busy, and that he must want her to rest; after a week, she had asked Sadie and Sadie had shrugged. The first morning she came downstairs to have breakfast, her father ate in silence then went outside without even looking at her, and although they rediscovered a little of their closeness as the years went by, they never did broach the subject of her 'illness'.

John had managed the orchard for a while after her father's death and then Jack had come along to help now and again, staying in an old caravan just inside the farm boundary when it suited him. Hannah had not looked after the orchard for a long time; to her, it had been more like an inanimate object, an obstacle she had to pass through. She raised her eyes and, as she did so, she realized the extent to which it had been neglected, the changes so slow that she had not noticed them. Today she could see the damage and the decay, the need for pruning, for stimulating growth. An orchard needed to be worked on; it could not be left or it would wind towards its own demise. A sudden grief settled upon her, nothing to do with John, but with the trees, and she felt an impulse to bring them back to her.

Hannah walked towards the old zinc shed where she hadn't been for a long time. She pushed open the warped door and pulled the light switch. Inside was the rusting machinery, the cider press and tools. Hannah thought a moment, then took a rake that was hanging from two nails in the wall and carried it out into the orchard. Starting with the oldest trees first, she began to rake away the dead leaves and windfalls – she did not want any diseases overwintering. After days in bed, the cold on her face felt refreshing. She felt the sharp air in her lungs, her fingers beginning to tingle, then her whole body warming with the exertion of pulling the rake through the long grass.

She worked until her back ached and the day began to open around her, the colour coming back to her cheeks, her eyes looking a little more alive. When she had finished, she took the rake back to the shed. As she hung it back on the wall, instinctively she looked up.

There, on the old wooden beams, her father had pencilled the names and genera of the trees in the orchard, acutely aware of the difference between his own longevity and that of the trees. There was a map of the orchard on the ceiling, constellations of trees studding the roof above her, a universe she had not chosen.

12

Smoke

There are some fears we carry within ourselves.
Perhaps some would call it instinct – that impulse to
reach out before a fall, self-preservation. Some fears are
older than that, even, are unconscious, innate. Bees are
afraid of fire, even if they have never seen it; they know
to be afraid of it, to fear it tearing through their nest.
I suppose this fear has come from millennia spent in
the forests, where the fittest survived by sensing smoke
early on. But how can we fear something we have
never seen, Hannah? How can we imagine the horrors
of something we don't even know? The beekeeper
harnesses this unconscious fear and turns it against the
hive. The smoke is a veil, concealing his manipulation,
a distraction that keeps the bees' attention elsewhere.

My father taught me how to walk the orchards
looking for old wood. Newspapers and pine cones
worked well, but the best thing for producing good
clean smoke was decayed wood. The kind that
crumbled under your fingers, had almost reverted to
soil. He gave me his old smoker, tarred black with oil
and heat over the years. He taught me how to control
the smoke, and its effects on the bees. If the fire is too
hot, it burns itself out before your work is done; if
it burns too cool, it isn't strong enough. You have to
cultivate the ability to manipulate it without fanning
the smoke into flame.

My father taught me how to open a hive, to stand behind it. To smoke the entrance as if you were a visitor, observing the niceties. It only takes a little smoke, and you can hear the immediate change of tone inside, a sudden preoccupation as the message is passed around that danger is near. Their innate response is to gather their stocks and prepare for flight to a safer place, where the honey that they bring with them will sustain them until they are established. The benefit of this to the beekeeper is that once a bee has a full abdomen, it can barely curve its body enough to sting you.

My father taught me to use a lot of smoke, for my own comfort, and when I was a young man, I saw nothing wrong with giving the bees a sense of danger, a routine uncertainty, the after-effects of which stayed with them for hours following each visit. In junior common rooms and public houses, the smoke from cigarettes would catch in my throat, each man egging the others on. As I grew older, I saw its cruelty. I see it now as an old man, but I did not see it then, Hannah. Perhaps it was my own failing, or perhaps it was the world which led me to believe that I was entitled to use any means within my power.

I am getting weaker, Hannah; I find writing difficult, the words trailing along these pages, but I wanted to say that I know in the past I used words that were thick with smoke, calculated. I could sense your unease when I went away with work and, in my stupidity and vanity, I would blow on the paper and control your murmurings. I think back on it with

shame. *I see how it permeated our marriage, Hannah,
how it set us apart. Your tense care for me before
I would leave, the palpable unspoken relief when I
returned. It blinded me, Hannah, to what we had;
I did not notice the thousand things that you did for
me. It seeped into my lungs so that I could not breathe.*

    *As I grew older, I found I used the smoker less and
turned to other ways of working with the bees. That
pillowcase you sewed for me, a rod at one end, draped
over the hive as I worked; a spray of sugar water to
keep them busy. But the most effective way, which
was not available to me, was to hide nothing from
them. They react to any agitation, any turbulence,
they draw it out of you and punish you accordingly,
and, although you may try to hide it, they can sense it
in the tremor of your hands and in the seeping of your
pores. In general, I think perhaps that is why older
beekeepers are sometimes better, because they become
more aware of their own failings and do not try to
hide them any more.*

    *As a young man, I did not see the subtleties; I was
drawn to lexicography and I would pursue the purity
of words, but the more I learnt, the more hopeless the
task seemed. Language is not stable; it is not a solid
but a gas, and we all use it selfishly. We bend it to our
will; we define it then abuse it. Sometimes I imagine
these books that surround me rising like smoke,
choking me as I sit. That is what happens when you
make a life from approximating life; you are never
burnt by the flame, but you are blinded by smoke.*

13

H ANNAH AND SADIE HAD begun collecting the firewood early, the sky above the orchard grey, matte and heavy with snow. The girl was supposed to come today and although it was mid-morning by now, it had barely become any lighter. It was bitterly cold, too, and Hannah wore her father's coat while they worked in complete silence, save for the sound of the wood hitting the wheelbarrow and the clack of Hannah stacking the logs in the shed. Jack had brought the wood before he left in autumn, but since John's illness it had lain in the open. Hannah stacked the wood against the zinc wall of the shed, barely able to feel her hands now. She had wrapped a thick scarf under the collar of the woollen coat, but her cheeks still stung.

Her mother had preferred ash for the fire, which her father would buy or trade for, even though they had a plentiful supply of fruit wood. She would not have elder anywhere near the log pile, though, for fear of drawing death to the house. Hannah could hear Sadie trimming the branches with an axe as she emptied the wheelbarrow and pushed it back outside. The sound was carrying far today, as it did in the cold. It was as if the sky was listening, every slice or cut amplified. It would be good to get the wood stored, separate out the kindling, ready for next year; it kept them busy so they did not have to feel the weight of their thoughts.

They worked their way through the pile, lifting,

splitting, tidying, and Hannah gathered any small twigs in a pile for burning. After they had finished, she went to the house and fetched some old newspaper and matches, pushed the paper under the bundle and brought a lit match to it. It was still today, the earth cold; it was safe to do this. Sadie came out of the shed and, as they watched the twigs spit in the gathering flames, the snow started falling. Large soft flakes descending slowly, silently, each one achingly cold, touching her face, catching in her hair. The light had now turned from grey to a deep blue. Sadie looked over at Hannah, who was standing by the stuttering fire, as the world changed colour around them. They waited for the fire to burn itself out before retreating to the house.

There, Sadie used last year's wood to light a fire and Hannah reheated some soup.

By early evening, they had wordlessly accepted that it would be unlikely that the girl would come today. The road from the village would be filled with snow by now, cutting off Berllan-Deg for goodness knows how many days – weeks, even. Sadie had thought that knowing this would relieve the tension for Hannah a little, but it only seemed to increase her irritation. Sadie had not seen Hannah make any preparations for the girl's arrival; she hadn't changed her clothes, even after clearing the wood, her hair was uncombed, and moss clung to the sleeves of her jumper. She had become increasingly quiet as the day drew on, as each snowflake made the orchard stiller. That was the thing about snow, thought Sadie: it seemed to conceal everything and reveal it at the same time, each footprint and path.

Her mind returned to the way her father used to follow her footsteps as she went to meet a friend when she was a young woman. His relief when he had realized that it was just a girl she was meeting. The pity she had felt for him, how he seemed to inhabit a world in which the truth did not even cross his mind. The girl she had met outside the town hall, shared a bottle of beer with while laughing at everyone inside; the girl who would ride her bike over to see Sadie, sit among the trees, the freckles on her shoulders like those on a blackbird's egg. She would light up when she saw Sadie, and that one gentle kiss, and then the cold, like snow, when she had had to move away from the town, leaving Sadie numb. She had told herself that it wasn't real, that her feelings were temporary, and, when she had left, like melted snow, there was no trace that anything had ever happened, save for Sadie's resolve to be more like her sister.

'I'm going to bed,' Hannah said suddenly. Sadie said nothing as she ascended the stairs and when she had heard Hannah's bedroom door close, she got up and opened the door and looked out at the falling snow. It had slowed now, the large flakes giving way to a silvery dust moving in every direction in the stillness. The tawny owls were calling tonight, their hearing sharpening in the silence. Sadie hadn't heard them for years. She felt the cold seep into her bones and closed the door.

14

FROM THE FEEL OF the light on her eyelids, Hannah could tell that it had snowed again through the night. Last night she had dreamt of him: they were both sitting at the table, and he was talking but she could not understand him. She thought of the letters that Sadie had placed in his desk drawer, her stomach churning at the memory of them. At first, she had baulked at the thought of reading them, and then she had found herself going to fetch them, grasping them in her hands. But the fear of what they might contain would then take hold and she could only bear to read a few lines before placing them back.

It was bright this morning in the kitchen, the house illuminated by the reflection of the snow. Sadie was asleep by the cold hearth; she had not moved since the night before. Hannah touched her hand and she stirred.

'I'll light the fire,' Hannah whispered. There was no firewood left so she moved to the doorway and pulled on her boots, threw a coat around her shoulders. As she stepped into the orchard, the air seemed to knife her. By its nature, the triangular orchard was sheltered, designed so that the winds would not blow through, taking with them the pollens in spring. It was a place where things settled, where snow lingered and the cold pooled. Hannah inhaled sharply, took the frigid air into her lungs and held the coat at the collar as she walked to the shed. She pushed at the door, found it stuck, so shouldered it open and had to wait as her eyes adjusted from the dazzle of the whiteness, listening to what sounded like a movement, a sudden gasp. Then she saw a figure, shifting, underneath a coat.

'I'm so sorry,' the girl said, getting up.

'What are you . . .?'

'I was trying to find . . .'

Hannah felt her breath leave her body as the outline of the girl's face seemed to sharpen in the gloom. Her eyes. They were devastating. It was like looking into his.

'I don't know if I'm in the right . . .'

Hannah felt her throat tighten. 'Yes,' she said starkly, 'you're in the right place.'

The girl had dark hair, was slight, and had the same way of holding her hands.

'I'm—' she began.

'I know who you are,' interjected Hannah.

'I'm . . . so cold,' she said.

Hannah took in her red-blue cheeks, the tips of her fingers.

'Of course,' she replied. 'You'd better come into the house.'

The girl nodded.

'I'm so sorry,' she said again.

Sadie was slow to react as Hannah brought her in. The young woman's hands seemed frigid, but there was a trembling in her that Sadie recognized as having nothing to do with the cold. Hannah closed the door behind them.

'I'm Megan,' the girl said quietly. 'I came by train, got a taxi from the town to the village; I thought there would be cars there, I didn't realize. I couldn't go back, and I didn't know where you were, I got so confused with the snow, and when I finally got here, it was so late I didn't want to knock.'

'You should have,' said Sadie, looking at Hannah. 'I'm so sorry.'

The girl's clothes were damp.

'I'll get you a blanket,' said Sadie, concerned.

'I'm fine,' replied Megan.

'Please, come and sit.'

Sadie gestured to the chair. Sadie and Hannah stood at the table in silence, each looking at the other in unspoken acknowledgement of how uncomfortable it was to see someone so familiar yet still a stranger.

Megan went to sit but then got back up again.

'I had planned what I was going to say,' she said, clearing her throat, 'but I didn't picture it like this.'

'Let me make you some tea, something to warm you up,' offered Sadie.

'No. No, thank you.' Megan smiled tensely. 'I know this is difficult.' She swallowed, as if her emotions were making her breathing shallow. 'I wanted to come because I thought it might help me and you . . . I thought . . .' She raised her eyes to meet Hannah's. 'If we can be open and clear . . . it helps everyone, doesn't it?'

Megan looked as if she did not quite believe her own words. She waited a few moments.

'The truth is that my mother told me that her encounter with my father was a mistake, that she did not love him. She raised me herself and told me that it was better if I accepted that I had no father.'

She looked away again, the conversation clearly a battle for her.

Hannah didn't take her eyes off the girl.

'You said he worked at the university?' Megan asked.

Sadie nodded.

'Languages?'

'Linguistics.'

Megan nodded, as if continuing a conversation with herself. 'Well, that would make sense. My mother . . .' At this, she stopped, her eyes darting towards Hannah. 'I'm sorry.'

Hannah cleared her throat. 'It's all right.'

'When I left home for college,' Megan continued, 'she married, had two more children. She was young when she had me . . . We don't speak much any more.'

Sadie could feel the sadness in the way Megan's gaze dropped on mentioning her mother.

'Her name is Nancy; she worked at the university for a while.'

Hannah said nothing, was numb.

'I suppose that's what you wanted to know.'

Sadie instinctively moved towards Hannah. Megan watched them.

'Is there anything else you want from me?' she asked, suddenly tearful.

Hannah was surprised by the question. 'I don't want anything from you.'

'Then why did you ask me to come?' Megan asked.

Hannah considered this. 'I wanted to see if it was true. I wanted to see with my own eyes, and now I can see that it is.'

Megan unknowingly placed her hands on the back of John's chair. Hannah's eyes dropped to the empty seat.

'I'd better get going,' Megan said.

Sadie looked at Hannah. She clearly did not understand.

'It's started snowing again,' said Sadie softly. 'You'll never get back to the village in this.'

Hannah gave a slight dip of her head. 'I'm afraid you won't be going anywhere for a while.'

Jack's caravan was cold, the door stiff from the damp. Inside, it was old-fashioned; a floral carpet and fringed curtains. There were a few books and carved objects and a lonely bed, along with a small wood-burning stove that was already laid with kindling.

'Are you sure you won't stay in the house?' Sadie said.

'I'll be fine here,' Megan replied, putting her bag on the bed. 'Thanks for the fresh clothes.'

'When you've changed, put your old ones in the bag, leave them on the step. I'll wash them and bring them back to you.'

Megan held her arm across her body, not knowing what to say.

'There's some tea here, too; I'm sure Jack won't mind. He works here in the summer,' Sadie offered. 'He's a bit nomadic. He won't be back until spring.'

Megan nodded.

'OK, then. I'll bring you some supper later on.'

'Thank you.'

Sadie turned to leave before pausing on the threshold.

'I'm sorry that this has happened to you,' she said, despite herself. 'It must have been a shock. I'm sure you understand that Hannah is still trying to come to terms with everything . . . on top of the grief, a lifetime's marriage and then this . . .'

Megan nodded, unsure what to say.

'Well,' smiled Sadie, 'I'll leave you to it.'

Megan tried to return the smile but was glad when Sadie left. She was exhausted. She stood for a moment feeling completely numb, before moving to the small stove and looking for some matches. There were spills already rolled from newspaper. She took one and lit it, watched as the kindling caught fire. She closed the stove door as the flames spread, not really feeling the tears on her face.

15

THE SNOW CLUNG on for days. Sadie had brought
Megan some food, a warm coat, a bag of fresh
kindling and her clothes, washed and pressed. Megan
had stayed in the caravan, sleeping on top of the bed-
clothes, and could hardly gauge how much time had
passed. This morning, the stove had been long since
extinguished, and the dropping temperature inside the
caravan must have woken her. She opened her eyes
and listened, still unused to the strangeness of being in
someone else's space.

She had been unsure whether to come at all, had
reread the letter from Sadie over and over. It had felt
like something she had been waiting for all her life, but
when it had finally come, its arrival had been abrupt and
she had not been ready for it. She had placed the letter
on the kitchen table and sat down to consider whether
she should call her mother. She had decided against it
eventually, unsure as to what she would discover; also,
her mother had made it abundantly clear that she had
little interest in Megan's real father, or sometimes even
in Megan herself. A friend at work had cornered her,
asked her why she was so quiet, but she had been able
to deflect, pretended she was just busy. She was long
practised in keeping people at arm's length.

She got up, pulled on the coat that Sadie had left
and walked to the road to see how deep the snow was.
It was completely silent. She turned her head, walked

down the lane in one direction only to find more and more anonymous lanes opening up as far as the eye could see. The cold was exquisite. No cars had passed for days and the only marks in the snow were her own footsteps and the alighting of birds. She turned back to get her bearings, tried to detect the location of the hedge along the road that obscured Berllan-Deg, centring herself.

She headed back into the orchard, past the caravan, and followed the boundary. The snow was deeper here and her steps were laboured. It occurred to her that, except for her neighbours or perhaps a colleague who might call over Christmas, no one would realize she was missing. She had cultivated a routine, the shared flat in which she hardly ever saw her flatmate, her job, the years passing in a haze of other people's celebrations. Polite conversations with colleagues, acquaintances, the partaking in life. The suffocating nights and the monotony of a rigid routine which she would not and did not feel able to break, the constant crippling anxiety that something was wrong. Sometimes on waking, she would run through everything and everyone she knew, and would be placated momentarily by the logic that everything was OK, that everyone was all right, but then the fear always started creeping back in. The sensations in her body that she didn't understand, the way she startled at the merest sound, and the breathlessness that left her feeling that she couldn't get enough oxygen out of the air.

She pushed on through the snow now, her coat open, really letting herself feel the cold. Her hair was greasy, and she knew she needed to wash, but she could not think of it.

In fairness, she had received a lukewarm invitation from an old friend for Christmas, but although she liked her immensely, they now had profoundly different lives. Her friend would be preoccupied with the children, with planning the next year's family holiday. Over the years, their conversations had thinned, curtailed by her friend's partner, and Megan would sit reading to the children, trying to find a way to make herself useful in order to assuage the guilt she felt for taking up space in their family time.

In the corner of the orchard there were a few shapes and she walked towards them. As she drew closer, she recognized them as hives, a few inches of snow on each one's roof. The snow was disturbed around them, compressed, and there were footsteps with no powder in the marks – someone had been there that morning. Megan put a foot in one. They were big, too; a man's, she'd guess. There were no other signs, just the footprints that had come in from the hedge by the road, circled the hives and retreated the same way. She looked back towards the house, but the snow through the orchard was pristine; it had not been anyone from there. There was smoke rising in a column from the chimney this morning, a sign that the weather would most likely be still for a while, and then she saw it: a face in the window. Megan squinted again, her stomach tightening, but it had gone. She realized that she could feel her heart in her chest, and she turned to move away, but as she did, her foot struck something metallic.

She looked down, cleared some snow with her numb fingers, and found an old iron key. She brushed it clean and warmed it in her palms a moment before slipping it into her pocket.

16

Cluster

You can pour bees like water. They are at once individuals and an entity. I have seen beekeepers manipulate them from vessel to vessel, and it is in wintering that this becomes more apparent. They lose interest in the world around them; their work is done, their harvest brought home. Their drive falls away, their ambition; their only instinct is to fold themselves around each other, keeping the queen at their centre. They ball around her to protect her in the heat of the hive and keep her warm, a mantle of older bees on the outside, the youngest bees nearest to her. She is their hope of establishing themselves once more in spring. Their lives depend on her survival.

To get through winter is difficult, and their calculations and preparations are tested to the limit. The stores they have accumulated, the warmth of the memories they have made; they seem to know that when winter comes, the outside world will not sustain them any more. They cannot become distracted by it; it is cold, unwelcoming.

These past few years have been our happiest, haven't they, Hannah? You must have felt that? Away from the distractions of the world, our lives stripped down to you and I. We have stored enough memories, haven't we? That summer we went to the coast, when the car got stuck in the sand. The dinners we went to. Your satin dresses. Those June days when we had to leave everything and rescue a swarm of bees from gardens here and there. The flasks of tea you made. And, lately, the nights we have sat in the orchard in silence, listening to the world turn.

The bees do not sleep, not like other creatures which hibernate – they merely begin to live more slowly, gathering closer when the coldest weather strikes, then loosening again, pulsing as winter rages around them. They are, in fact, a heartbeat, slower than in summer, but steadier, self-sufficient, in tune with each other.

Tonight, you looked tired, Hannah; you went to bed early and I came here to write. My sleep is getting worse – isn't that strange? You would think that I would become sleepier. I think of the memories I have, the ones you have, and wonder how they differ. I torment myself that they will not be enough to keep you warm.

My cluster is final, Hannah; I do not think that a new spring awaits me, but I feel that you will have many more. That one day soon, you will sense the slice of a stem through the cold soil. The first flowers. That you will feel the call of smudged pollen, and the hard buds of the hazel trees. I fear what I have done, I fear that it will deaden that impulse for you to inhale sharply at the end of winter, to look up and out. I fear that I will not be here to help you.

I was selfish, Hannah, to keep you at the centre, in order to enjoy our wintering. I want you to know that there have been nights when I have felt so cold *and the horror of my actions has made me shut the door fast and turn towards the fire. There have been days when I have wandered the lanes and resolved to come back to tell you, but then I have seen your happiness. I have felt it, and I would have shattered that; I would have changed everything for something that could not be changed.*

17

H ANNAH HAD WOKEN EARLY, her thoughts circling around Megan: the way she tilted her head to listen, her gestures, each one an echo. Her aching familiarity and her shocking unfamiliarity and those eyes. Hannah felt full to the brim, the emotion threatening to spill over so that she found it difficult to breathe. She felt weak but she needed to move, so she pulled on her trousers and her jumper, walked down the stairs and went out into the orchard, the morning light dazzling on the snow.

She stopped for a moment, exhaled, saw her breath in the cold air, evidence that she was still alive. Her heart began to slow and her stomach softened. She had lain in bed last night, thoughts of Megan plaguing her, but then the trees had come to her again. Images of them. Dormant, their leaves fully gone, the sap inside them still and, for a second time, she'd felt that impulse grow within her.

It was about time; the trees were years overgrown, had been left to their own devices, and Hannah did not know if they were salvageable at all. When she was a child, her father had taught her how to look at a tree, to examine its shape and recognize how to cut it back. The art was to stress the tree, to threaten its very existence so that it redoubled its resolve to survive. To wake it from its self-absorbed stupor and maim it in a way that would make it think about growth. The advantage of cutting the tree in the snow would be that the wound would not bleed as much. They were as dormant as they would ever be at this time of year.

Armed with her father's loppers, Hannah looked at the tree in front of her. It was not about what you cut, but what you left behind and the potential of that. The trees weren't tall, having been kept small so that the apples would be easily accessible, their fruit low-hanging. She surveyed this first tree, tried to see what was hidden in its shape, then she raised the loppers and made the first cut, her breath billowing in the air. The smell of the wood struck her. She needed to make room, find the negative space. She cut again, with more difficulty this time as the branches had grown thick.

The thing about the trees was that they were never just trees, they were a collection of co-dependent organisms; they hosted birds, insects, blooms and fungi. They were home to mosses and lichens, each one a universe. As they aged, they could become weighed down with their dependents and forget about revitalizing themselves. The best thing to try to do was to feel your way to what you were trying to achieve, find your way towards it. She cut another branch and watched as it fell on to the pristine snow.

She was getting warm now as she tried to cut a thicker branch only to fail. She swore under her breath, frustrated at her own weakness. She went to fetch a handsaw, her boots sinking in the snow. When she came back, she found her sister among the fallen branches. She looked at her, smiled tensely.

'I think I've left it too long,' Hannah said. She looked pained.

Sadie noticed that her sister was breathing heavily. 'I don't think so,' she answered. Hannah frowned, then walked back towards the branch she wanted to cut. She marked it with a rasp or two of the blade before beginning to saw.

Instinctively, Sadie started to help. She bent over and dragged the branches into a pile, clearing the way after Hannah had cut. And, like this, they worked for hours with nothing but the sound of the saw and the thud of each branch as it fell. The folds of Hannah's jumper filled with sawdust, and her arms burnt.

Sadie pulled another branch across the orchard, brushing new shapes into the snow, her mind retreating to a few weeks ago, the brushing of fingers over her back. Her limbs were loosening as her muscles warmed up, this new awareness that she had of herself still growing. On those few days before John died, before any of this, she had met her body, for the first time, under a woman's hands. Had found herself both disorientated and filled with sensation as never before. Those long years with her husband, then those two days with the woman, and she had flinched, both from her uncertainty and from the power of it. She had driven home to find the message from Hannah and had had to put all such thoughts aside. The fact that she had not told the woman that she was going home, and then the orchard, seeing once again all the things that had formed her, made her realize how fractured she still was. How difficult it was going to be to piece herself back together.

John had known. Being a little older, perhaps, he

had become suspicious of Sadie and her friend and had confronted her, and she had hated him for it. Not because she had feared what he would do – he had been considerate and kind, promised he would never betray her trust – but because she felt violated; because he had laid bare this fumbling newness in her, and had exposed it to a glare that it could not withstand. The only advice he had given her was that she would not be accepted at Berllan-Deg or in this community, that if she wanted to be free to live her life, she would have to leave. She had begrudgingly agreed that he was telling the truth.

Hannah and Sadie had not worked in such harmony for years, each one reading the other, acknowledging the other's tiredness. Coming back to the trees, older. Hannah looked up at the last tree. It was too crowded in the centre. The broad shape you were looking for was a chalice, a cup. No branches should touch or rub – there should be no places where friction could cause damage; you had to cut away disease and rot, anything that could fester, and make sure that any buds and eventually the fruit would be exposed to the sun. Hannah tried to imagine the tree within the tree. She cut once more, each removal a relief, found herself focusing on something she could not yet see. An emerging idea that needed destruction to bring it to light.

18

J ACK HAD LEFT A pheasant on the doorstep, its mouth agape, a few smears of dark-red blood on the snow. Hannah looked at it, its bright plumage startling against the monochrome orchard. Jack often brought gifts, and it was best not to ask where he'd got them. She picked it up and carried it to the kitchen table.

She had not been surprised when he had not come to the funeral; it would have been too formal for him, and Hannah knew that he would have found his own way to say farewell to John. That was Jack's nature; he would not conform in the ways you expected him to, but would show his respect through his continued care for the bees, the carrying of firewood into the shed and, in summer, the leaving of a river-damp trout wrapped in newspaper on the kitchen bench. Words meant nothing to Jack, Hannah knew that, and she would not question the depth of his grief even though she knew that John's death would probably never be mentioned by him.

Hannah fetched some newspaper and laid it on the kitchen table, then took the empty ash bucket from the fireplace. She began plucking the pheasant. It had been hung; she could tell by the ease with which the feathers came away. She pulled at the tail feathers and the wingtips where the quill feathers were, before working on the down. She began to fill the bucket, flicking her damp fingers so that the feathers wouldn't stick to them and trying not to rip the breast of the bird as she worked. When she had finished, she severed the head, cut the legs and pulled away the knee sinews with them. Then she stuck the knife into the bottom of the bird's abdomen, pushed in her fingers and gutted it, throwing the entrails on to the feathers in the bucket. She placed the bird on a platter and went to wash her hands. It would be ready for Christmas Day tomorrow.

Jack had lived with his mother in the village until he was around seventeen and had come asking for work. Hannah had looked at him over John's shoulder. He was gaunt, in the way that only a boy rapidly growing into a man can be, his checked shirt too big for him. She had noticed the way he did not want to meet her gaze. John had taken pity on him, offered him some work with little expectation, but the boy had thrived, had found a love for the trees and taken in every instruction in a way he apparently never had at school. He never seemed to tire of stacking wood, and was taught how to put up fencing and, eventually, to look after the bees.

At this time of year he would usually be laying hedges, and could often be found by a roadside somewhere, the van in which he slept near by, a sign placed on the road in case any passing traffic required his skills. There was always a look of quiet contemplation as he cut the saplings with a billhook, deep enough that they would become pliable, but not deep enough to kill them. He would then weave them together, working with the nature of the hedge while allowing the wood enough room for growth. In spring he would start checking the hives again and, in this way, he had carved out a life, a rhythm which followed the seasons. He had been the closest Hannah and John had had to a child, and he had eaten with them, and would sometimes leave a shirt or some clothes that had caught in the brash for Hannah to repair.

At first she and John had adjusted to his presence by speaking English when he was around, although he never minded if they unconsciously slipped into Welsh when talking to each other. He seemed to sense the effort they were making for him. John had had to teach him to care for the bees through Welsh, though, as it was the only language he associated with them. Over the years Jack had absorbed enough to understand if not always speak it, and their intimacy as a three had grown so that the long conversations Hannah and John had in Welsh were simply a sign that they were less self-conscious around him. Hannah would watch Jack and, despite sometimes sitting on the periphery of talks, the language was not excluding him; it seemed to be embedding him.

It was strange now to have another presence in the orchard, to know she was there. The plates that Sadie carried back and forth, her clothes drying on the stove. Hannah had picked them up, felt their weight in her hands. She had seen Megan by the hives one evening, and had wondered how the girl viewed the orchard and Berllan-Deg in the snow, as someone so wholly new to it. For a moment, she had envied her for that.

Hannah dried her hands now, set to work on some vegetables that she would leave in pans of water ready for tomorrow. When she was a child, Christmas had been spent in chapels singing Plygain. Her father would scrawl a list in pencil on the back of a crinkly envelope of the services he wished to attend. He would practise with some men from the village, and then the season would start. The gathering in chapels to sing ancient carols; her father in his suit, her mother clutching her patent handbag. It would be cold, so cold, but then there was the singing. The services were informal, and the reverend would invite anyone who wished to sing to do so. There would be no accompanying music and the majority sang in groups, sometimes travelling from one chapel to another. The singing was a conversation, an exploration of the language of worship. If, by chance, someone else had performed the carol you intended to sing, then you had to change your song, meaning that your depth of knowledge was tested, the breadth of your study highlighted. Her mother would sit, her eyes closed, listening, her mind somewhere else. Hannah would watch the singers, Sadie's head invariably leaning on her shoulder. Often, they weren't particularly gifted singers or ones used to performing; they were farmers, teachers, shopkeepers, all singing together. The closer the harmonies, the more the sound seemed to hum around the chapel, making the old building come alive. The thing that Hannah remembered most, though, was that there would be no applause, that sometimes she would forget herself and raise her hands to clap before remembering the ingrained lesson that pleasure should not necessarily be articulated, that it could be felt.

They would walk home, Sadie running ahead in the snow, jumping into areas where there were no footprints, and Hannah would lag behind, watching her father, his age beginning to show in his gait, his arm entwined with her mother's, making sure that she didn't slip. Hannah used to look at the silhouette of her mother's two-piece outfit and hat, and wonder whether this was what marriage would look like for her.

She and John had attended Plygain, too, her mother on John's arm, her father having just passed; her mother sitting next to John, silent tears wetting her face. Over the years, as the old people died out, the chapel congregation had dwindled, and as neighbouring farms and smallholdings were sold, fewer and fewer attended. The incomers would be friendly people, of course, but then again, cultures were often suffocated by kind people. She would not think of attending today, even though the service was still being held, because the remaining attendees would know by now – about Megan, and about John. Hannah had nothing to feel shame about, but she harboured an intense irritation that she would be a talking point.

She heard Sadie's footsteps on the staircase behind her.

'She isn't what I thought she'd be,' Sadie said, joining her. 'I think she looks a little sad, a little lonely.'

Hannah had been thinking this, too.

'The snow can't last much longer, surely,' said Sadie under her breath.

'Three months has been the longest,' answered Hannah, crossing her arms.

'Well, let's hope it's not that long, for her sake.'

*

Hannah had always made the Christmas wreaths, gathering greenery from the orchard. This afternoon, she had looked over at the caravan and made sure there was no movement before taking some old sewing scissors and going outside. She would have to be quick, did not want Megan to witness her private ritual. Ivy grew strongly here, seemed to enjoy wrapping its poisonous heart-shaped leaves around the borders of the orchard, and there was plenty of glossy holly resplendent with berries. Hannah cut as efficiently as she could before carrying armfuls back into the house and trying to disentangle the greenery from her jumper.

Hannah went to find some old wire coat hangers, some scissors and twine. She wound the wire into circles before beginning work. Sadie came to the table to sit, watched as Hannah made a wreath for their parents. She had picked some mistletoe, which grew in untidy clumps on the apple trees. Sadie felt the milky berries between her fingers for a moment, looked at the sage-coloured leaves.

'Do you remember us pressing these berries into the bark of the trees? Trying to get them to take hold?'

Hannah smiled.

'We were so excited at the thought of growing up.'

Hannah started to wind some moss on to the wire. 'John used to help me gather the mistletoe on a sheet. There was so much of it, it was a strain on the trees. We'd leave it out on the road for anyone who wanted it.'

Sadie could hear the warmth of Hannah's memories in her voice, looked at the mistletoe in her fingers. 'Did you forgive him back then?' she asked suddenly, finding it easier to push the words out into the open now their hands were occupied.

'For what?'

'For . . . you know . . .'

'Say it.'

'For leaving you to cope when he went away to university. It's just that we never spoke about it.'

Hannah picked up some holly, felt it needling the skin of her hands. 'You were too young for me to talk to,' she said.

'But I understood,' said Sadie.

'Did you?'

'I had to pretend I didn't.'

Hannah considered her sister. 'He was not much more than a child himself. Of course, I forgave him. His father was furious. His mother, too. I never liked her.'

Sadie smiled.

'The older we became and the more we grew up together, the more I thought about how young we had been and how much we had trusted the world to look after us.'

'You see, I couldn't,' said Sadie. 'I couldn't forgive him. I didn't dislike him; it was just that I couldn't forgive him. It was just that you were so alive – you have no idea how alive you were back then, so full of everything, of life, of . . .' Sadie ran out of words. 'You could have done anything, gone anywhere, had anyone, but he . . .'

'He what?' Hannah raised her voice a little.

Sadie searched her face, trying to work out how honest she could be. 'Nothing.'

'He held me back?'

'I didn't say that. It was just that something changed in you.'

'Did you ever consider him? The sacrifices he made?'

Sadie looked confused.

Hannah put down her work, pressed her palms against the surface of the table. Tried to keep her voice even.

'I saw the belt marks on his body, Sadie. I didn't see the bruising – that was gone by the time we married – but the scars were still there. Imagine how hard he was hit for the buckle to leave marks that lasted a lifetime.'

Sadie felt a rush of tears. 'You never told me that,' she said.

'Perhaps I should blame our parents, his parents? Perhaps I should blame everyone in the village because they were the ones who made our parents feel ashamed. But it was a different time,' Hannah added. 'Then you stopped coming home.'

'You didn't really want me here,' Sadie said, a cold laugh stopping abruptly in her throat. 'Seth didn't want to come . . .'

'Was it Seth or was it you?' asked Hannah gently. 'It was lonely, you know.' There was a seriousness to Hannah now, as if she had to drag the words out. 'Looking after Mother wasn't the easiest. You never came home; you left me with her.'

Sadie could not look at her sister, could not answer.

'I did my best every day, Sadie, but nothing, *nothing* was ever good enough for her.'

'Listen, I'm sorry,' Sadie said, a little too curtly.

Hannah looked crestfallen, old questions forming in her mouth.

'I just couldn't come back,' said Sadie, her eyes roaming the room.

'But why?' asked Hannah.

Sadie twisted the greenery tightly.

'Because . . . because this place, this . . .'

Hannah looked at her in bewilderment.

'It's just the way I feel when I'm here . . . it's . . .'

Hannah waited, but Sadie said no more.

'You left, you got married, you didn't come home and then, out of the blue, you left Seth. I mean, it looked like a good marriage, from what I saw of it?'

'It was.'

'Then why?'

Sadie shrugged. 'Because something was missing, because I was suffocating, because I was lonely.'

Hannah looked up at this.

'And you're happier now? Sadie?'

Sadie felt the words form in her mouth, felt their shape but could not speak them.

Hannah waited before exhaling loudly. She had secured the moss around her wreath, and now she began to weave in the ivy, slowly, fastening it with twine until she had finished. She placed the completed wreath on the table, took hold of a new wire circle and paused, thinking about how she would go about making a wreath to remember John. Sadie watched her, the way Hannah's hands hovered between mistletoe and holly.

'Mistletoe is poisonous, you know,' Sadie said wryly. Hannah laughed sadly, then slowly reached out across the table and squeezed Sadie's hand.

At dusk, the two sisters walked down the lane towards the cemetery. It was getting dark, but it felt freeing to be away from the orchard for a while, away from the caravan, the house. The chapel loomed in the distance; the ground around it covered in snow. They wound their way along the footpath, left clear in a few places under the dense shelter of yew trees, and found the graves. Sadie laid down the wreath for their parents, and Hannah stood holding hers for a while. There was no stone for John yet, only a pile of earth, raw and untidy. She gasped, partly from the cold, and partly because she had not been prepared for coming back here. Sadie took her arm, and they stood in the deep-blue evening, their stinging arms and scratched hands a reminder of the pain of remembrance.

19

Sol-fa

One of my earliest memories is sitting under the organ at the chapel as my mother pedalled it into life. The sound encircling me as those heavy notes billowed and bellowed into the empty chapel. She would practise for hours, and I would sit, breathing in those chords. When I was older, she would give me the hymn board and a box of numbers for me to practise my maths as she played. It was her only place of peace, somewhere for her to find respite from the washing, the cooking.

As I got older, I could not listen to music like that any more. I rationalized it; I judged it, I suppose, preferring the hits we danced to in the town hall, the classical music my tutors admired. The ability to feel music has come back to me lately, with the weakening of my eyes, and in these past few years I have noticed so many things I was blind to.

When a queen has left a hive or is dead, you can hear it in the bees' dissonance. She is, if you like, the conductor, her movements perplexing, seemingly in front of or behind the beat, but she in fact sets the tone and pace for everyone. Sometimes, when bad weather is coming, the tone changes, and I have heard that bees can predict death, too, although I am not sure.

Do you know, when I began keeping bees, I would steal the offertory envelopes, those small paper squares we gave money to the chapel in, and

I would fill them with sugar or thyme, whatever the bees needed. My mother was apoplectic, firstly because without the envelope, the amount she had given would be known by all, and secondly because she was adamant that I would never get to heaven if I offered my worship to the bees instead of God. Perhaps I should have felt guilty, but nothing gave me greater pleasure than opening the hive a week later and finding that the bees had eaten through the paper with its brittle printed cross.

I could not find the solace our parents found in those cold chapels, Hannah. I could not sit for an hour at a time, my hands freezing and my back stiff, waiting for it to be over. Perhaps we should not have been married there, but how could we not have been? My mind hasn't been changed by age, either, as it is for so many. We need something – as creatures, we need something – but I don't think it is religion, Hannah. My father used to believe that if we did not live in fear of something, then there would be no order, but what if we lived in wonder instead?

It is only lately that I have come to hear the music of the hive. It's sol-fa, each gesture a note, a message conveyed. The stanzas and codas. I will never forget the fear I felt the first time my father allowed me to open a hive full of bees. A primal fear that walked the length of my young spine and spread across my skin, and, after feeling that weakness, that helplessness, I resolved never to feel it again. To do everything I could to control the bees. Their sounds felt intoxicating, dangerous. And it did not use to trouble me to open a *hive that sounded unhappy. If I had thought to open it that day, then I would. I did not have the time nor the inclination to wait. I had seen older beekeepers place their palms on the crown boards of hives after taking off the roof and listen, letting the note of the hive run through them; and if that note wasn't happy, they would replace the roof, leave the hive alone and respect the bees' wishes. It took me many years to learn that particular lesson. That warnings could be given silently, that permission needed to be voiced.*

It's said that bees received their sting from the God of Thunder in return for their honey, but that the condition for being given the means to protect themselves was that their sting would be fatal only to themselves. A queen's barb is longer than a worker bee's, and curved, and it can only be used to kill another queen. She is designed to be less indiscriminate, only to kill when her life is in danger. Male bees do not have stings at all. Nature does not trust them with poison.

These last few years, I have heard hymns in hives, Hannah. I have been thinking about them lately. Solemn songs, and songs of joy. The last time I opened a hive, it was midsummer, and, preoccupied with their work, they were placid, gentle. I cannot tell you, Hannah, how beautiful it was. The power of their assonance released something in me, drew tears I did not know were there. Like the first time we were together, Hannah, it was as if I had touched life itself.

20

CHRISTMAS DAY DAWNED FRIGID and bright, the snow still stubbornly maintaining its grasp on the orchard. A cold sun on Christmas Day was thought to bring good luck to the apples and a plentiful harvest. That's what their father used to say: that the trees needed cold temperatures in order to produce blossom. Hannah remembered thinking how strange it was that they would need something so harsh to produce something so delicate.

Hannah went downstairs early to put on the vegetables and light the fire.

'We can't leave her in the caravan today,' Sadie said as she entered the kitchen.

Hannah ignored her and went to fill the kettle.

'Hannah?'

'Perhaps she should have thought of that before coming here in the snow.'

'Hannah . . .' Sadie admonished.

The kettle was spitting on the hotplate, and Hannah turned to place the pheasant in the oven. She stood awhile, knowing her sister was right, her hand still on the stove.

Sadie went to fetch Megan at midday. At first, Megan had been unsure whether to accept the invitation, but she was beginning to feel the claustrophobia of the caravan bearing down on her and had thought that perhaps a few awkward hours outside it might be better than sitting alone within it. Sadie led her to the house and waited as she pulled off her boots at the door. Hannah had laid the table.

'Come and sit down,' said Sadie, as Hannah doled out the food. There wasn't much but it was enough. Megan sat quietly, but noticed that Hannah had yet to look at her.

'Your family must be missing you today,' Sadie ventured.

'Of course,' Megan answered, picking up her knife and fork.

They ate in silence for a moment, but Sadie could never abide silence.

'And you've got a partner, a husband?'

Megan shook her head. She did not offer anything more so Sadie went back to eating. Megan tried to eat, to swallow, but was feeling increasingly warm and uncomfortable. She had somehow become used to the coolness of the caravan over the past few days.

'And what do you do?'

Megan took a sip of water. Sadie noticed the hand that held her glass was unsteady.

'I work in a small museum,' she said. 'I make up the exhibitions.' They fell into another uncomfortable silence, the minutes dragging by.

'Oh for goodness' sake,' said Hannah, getting up abruptly, 'there's no heat in this fire today.'

Megan flinched on hearing the scrape of Hannah's chair, her frame sprung tight. She listened as the older woman threw another log on the fire, the burning wood collapsing down on itself. She could hear Sadie making small talk about the pheasant and how her father used to snare rabbits around the orchard, but her voice was indistinct. Megan tried to concentrate on her food but it seemed to stick in her throat. She put down her knife and fork.

Hannah began to clear the plates away, a coldness in her every gesture.

'I'll be going as soon as it thaws,' Megan declared suddenly.

'There's no rush,' interjected Sadie.

Megan half smiled. Exhaled sharply. 'I think we all know that there is. The thing is that you've lived with the uncertainty for only a few weeks, but I've spent my whole life not knowing,' she continued. 'I've been feeling angry with him, too.'

Hannah stopped washing the dishes. 'It doesn't seem to make much sense to be angry with someone you didn't know.' Her voice was clipped.

'He took away my chance of knowing him.'

Hannah still had her back to Megan.

'There's no one to blame for this,' Megan said. 'It took two of them, and my mother wasn't married . . .'

At this Hannah turned around sharply.

'But she must have known *he* was married,' she said. 'She was young—'

'And that was an excuse, was it?' Hannah interrupted.

'I'm not saying that.'

The fire had started to take hold now.

'It was *him* – he did this to you and me. He had the power and now you're blaming her?' Megan got up. 'I think this was a mistake.'

'Megan, please.' Sadie held out a hand.

'It's too much for you, and maybe it's too much for me,' Megan said, her words curt.

'I've been trying to rationalize it, to think why he would have behaved in the way he did. Why he only admitted to it now, why he'd do this to me and you?'

Hannah searched her face.

'I don't understand it,' Megan continued. 'It feels cruel, pointless. I don't know why he couldn't just say—'

'I couldn't have children,' blurted Hannah. Megan looked as if she had been hit.

'I couldn't have children,' Hannah repeated, more softly now. 'I wouldn't tell anyone usually, but I think in this case . . .'

There were tears in Megan's eyes now. She nodded.

'I'm sorry about that,' she said, her voice breaking.

Hannah felt exposed and her irritation flamed once more.

'I don't need your sympathy – I have come to terms with it – but it felt . . . he knew that . . .'

'That's why he didn't tell you?' asked Megan.

'I don't know. Perhaps.'

'I don't need anything from you,' Megan said. 'What I did need was for him to care enough about me to say something to either of us when he was alive.'

She stood in silence for a moment.

'With the thaw, I'll be gone and you can put all this behind you – we both can.'

Hannah nodded and, with that, Megan turned and walked out.

21

False Spring

The bees are at their most vulnerable not in the depths of winter but in the tentative spring. I have seen so many hives survive the darkest and coldest months to perish only weeks from salvation. You know, Hannah, there is no silence like the silence of a dead hive; it is quieter than death, more profound than stillness. To open a hive in the harsh spring light and see the black cluster, their bodies still packed tightly together, and to have to empty it out on to the cold earth – it is the most disheartening thing. For it is not the cold that kills them, but hope. A few days of warm weather, a respite from the cold, and they are so eager to believe in spring that they embrace it wholeheartedly. They reach for something that is not real. Having loosened up their cluster, the cold returns and they cannot warm up again. Their movements become slower, and death seems to seep like a liquid into the hive.

She was a false spring, a hope that wasn't real. We met when the precariousness of our winter was coming to an end. My mistake was not to turn myself back towards you. It was not her fault, just a strange fleeting warmth that I thought might be a cure. A brush, a mere brush, and I cannot forgive myself. I do not deserve forgiveness and it infuriates me how you and I yearned for, longed for, a child. Your dark desperation. The years and years of lying together, the months and months and months, and then all it took was a brush. No more than the alighting of a bee on a flower.

You were older then, and we could no longer think of a child, which seemed to settle things for you. The agonizing possibility was removed, the end of treatments, and, with that, you seemed to sleep easier, but I would lie awake next to you. I knew everything had changed, that it would never be the same, but I could not shatter you. I thought that I could leave it until tomorrow and tomorrow and tomorrow. You must understand that I would have told you anything but this? When you had already suffered enough. And I have wondered over the years if you would have been happier if you had known, if in time you would have forgiven me. If you could have found happiness elsewhere. But you were happy, weren't you, Hannah? I think you were. I felt it. We were both happy.

I have noticed that when a bee emerges in spring and begins to harvest pollen from a flower, it will stay faithful to that kind of flower. It is as if it has spent time learning the flower's structure, its curves, the intricacies of that bloom, and does not wish to begin again. It will visit the flower over and over and the flower will look after it, not attracting it with nectar if it is cold or raining, knowing that it needs the bee as much as the bee needs it. The bee, in turn, tends to the flower with a breath-taking intensity, until, at the end of its life, it still flies to it, its wings ragged. How wise they are, Hannah.

There have been changes, Hannah, in the warmth of spring. The world, it seems, has become more difficult for bees to navigate. There are dry summers and long wet autumns, winters that do not cool. The bees have relied in the past on an innate knowledge, a feeling for the seasons, but now they have none and I wonder if they yearn for those former times. When they could know, when they had certainty, and could feel safe and capable. I imagine they do.

22

MEGAN LAY IN THE bed and listened. She was getting used to the rhythms of the orchard around the caravan and was sure the snow was beginning to thaw; she could hear the occasional clump falling past the window. The caravan was also more familiar to her, and she experienced a strange possessiveness at the thought that she would soon leave it, and that the man would come back. She had been guessing what he was like, was used to looking for clues, had even made a living from it. At the museum, she would compile scenes, tableaux of lives lived so people could imagine stepping into them. An old cottage or a kitchen, each one meticulously researched and put together, but she was always astonished how difficult it was to feign life. To make a place look inhabited, the way people used the objects around them. Jack's clothes were plain, well made in the first place then mended. There were only a few of them stacked in the drawers next to the bed. There was coffee, tea and a small number of books. She had looked at them over the past weeks; there was no fiction, no novels, only books of facts, encyclopaedias. A couple of books on woodworking, hedge-laying and reference books, about birds, woodland moths and butterflies.

It was not until she had come to Berllan-Deg that she had realized the cacophony of birds that existed. She had read about their calls, their markings and habits.

At home she would have been blind to them, but here they were insistent, vibrant. It was the great tits that began singing first every morning, a kind of see-saw call, then the robins, then wrens and chiffchaffs. She would lie, trying to identify them, her eyes closed, her whole body listening, and sometimes she would even go back to sleep before reawakening, her head full of birdsong. When she heard the clink of the plate that Sadie left each morning on the step outside, she would open the door and take a slice of bread, spreading the crumbs across the snow, then watch motionless as the birds' hunger drew them close. Over the days, she became sure that they were calculating the danger she posed, through their cocked heads and their continued assessment of her. She thought it must be late now, as the chiffchaffs were calling, but there was a different sound, too, a clattering. She turned her head. There it was again.

Megan swung her legs over the side of the bed and drew on her trousers. The enamel bowl she had filled with water to wash in was still on the floor in front of the wood burner. She pulled on her boots and Sadie's coat and opened the door. The noise again. She followed it along the hedgerow, noticing as she did that there had not been any new snowfall.

There was a figure by the hives. Tall, a man, his shoulders slightly rounded. He was sliding his hand under a hive as if trying to get a sense of its weight. She approached, and although she was sure he could hear her, he didn't react. He let the hive down gently and walked to the next, before bending down once more and pressing his head to it, listening then tipping it gently to one side. He straightened up, looked dissatisfied, and pulled an old canvas sack towards him. Megan stood watching him.

'Hold this, will you?' he asked, offering her the bag. His hair was dark, the colour of ash around his temples, three deep laughter lines an accent to the corners of his hazel eyes. She held the bag as he took what looked like a long blade from it and began to loosen the top of the hive.

'Won't they come out?' asked Megan in alarm.

He carried on, half smiling. She heard a crack as he lifted off the roof.

'They're a bit short of honey; they'll have made their way through their stores in this cold weather.'

He placed the roof on the ground, reached out a hand for the bag. Megan stepped forward and he rummaged in the sack before finding what he needed. A heavy yellow square that looked a little like icing. He laid it inside the top of the hive.

'What is it?'

'Sugar,' he replied, wiping his fingers on his trousers. 'It's not the best way, but it'll keep them alive, hopefully.'

Megan watched as he replaced the roof.

'I'm—'

'I know who you are,' he interrupted, squaring off the top of the hive. 'You're the caravan thief.'

Megan's face fell.

'I'm so sorry, I didn't . . .'

He laughed now, his eyes creasing.

'You're John's daughter,' he said steadily. 'That's what they're saying.'

She had never heard herself described in that way before. He continued to the next hive, hefted its weight.

'News travels fast around here,' he said, the strain of holding up the hive in his voice.

'That one should make it through,' he mumbled, then he looked at her properly.

'You really are his daughter, aren't you?'

Megan looked away. 'I wouldn't know.'

Jack pointed at the hives with the blade.

'These were your father's. His apiary. His hives,' he said.

Megan's eyes were drawn to them.

'He taught me. I wouldn't usually check on them much at this time of year, but they sometimes struggle when their owner dies.'

Megan frowned. 'Why?'

'I don't know. It breaks their hearts, I guess. Grief? They know more than we do.'

Megan felt a sudden panic at the thought of the bees dying before spring.

'Is there anything else we can do to help them?'

'I've done all I can,' Jack said as he started to walk away.

Megan felt her anxiety grow.

'When will you be back?'

'I don't know,' he answered, his voice getting quieter. 'When it's time. In the meantime, enjoy my caravan!'

He turned and disappeared through a gap in the hedgerow, out into the lane.

Megan waited for the quiet to settle back on the orchard, then tentatively stretched out her hand and laid it on one of the hives. She closed her eyes, bent down and put an ear to the hive, exactly as Jack had done, and listened to the world within.

23

H ANNAH HAD KEPT TO herself since Christmas Day.
Sadie knew it wasn't intentional; it was just her
sister's way when she was hurt. Sadie had tried to keep
herself occupied, but Hannah's detachment unsettled
her and she decided some fresh air might change her
mood. As she closed the door behind her, she looked
across at the caravan. It was quiet there, too.

It had been a defining feature of her life, the sense of
being pushed to the edge; she had felt it when she was
a small child, trying to ingratiate herself with Hannah.
And then as she grew, trying to take the other girls' cues
at school, laughing at the things they laughed at, feign-
ing interest in the things they liked doing. Hannah,
despite being less social than Sadie, had more of an ease
somehow.

Sadie followed the path through the trees and down
towards the lane. The snow was getting muddier now,
more opaque. Sadie knew these lanes well, but somehow they looked different now. There were physical
differences – the blocking up of a gate here or there, or
the felling of a tree she remembered – but it was something more than that. She continued down the lane,
walking in the middle of the road, but despite knowing
that no one would come, she still felt uneasy.

Her husband had had a knack for making her talk
a lot, to overcompensate. It hadn't been a bad marriage;
he hadn't done anything wrong. It was in his silences,

though. The way he'd get up sometimes in the middle of the night, sit on the edge of the bed, a profound sadness about him, refusing to talk. The way he'd flick his hand in irritation at the slightest thing, which made Sadie try to fill every moment with warmth – such a desperate warmth. It had been exhausting, however, and the thing that had made it most difficult to bear was the fact that she was the root of his restlessness, his dissatisfaction; it was just that she hadn't ever admitted it to herself.

Sadie walked around the bend and could see the village in the distance, the church at its centre, a few houses. She stopped at the stone bridge and looked at the river running under it, remembered the paper boats she used to make as a child. They had been friends, good friends, they had grown up together, travelled a fair bit, but just as he had sensed that something was missing in their marriage, she had, too, and it wasn't affection or sex or anything tangible, it was just that, like that fallen tree in the orchard, there was someone else inside her taking root.

At the sign to the village she stood a moment. The panorama of her childhood looked so small. They had walked to school here, Hannah pulling her hand impatiently as she took her to the village primary school before catching the bus to the big school. From here, too, they had travelled to the nearest town, ten miles away, to go to dances and the cinema. A life she barely recognized now. It was quiet today, only the vague sound of children playing in the snow. She turned and walked back towards Berllan-Deg.

She had known that when she left her husband, he would never speak to her again. That he would not be able to accept it, that their friends would not accept it, and for the most part she had been right. They had no children, but she had had to pick apart their lives at the seams for her own sanity and, because of that, she had to destroy his. It was not intentional, it was not a deception, it wasn't any of those things, but it still cut both of them to the quick. And she missed him still, and sometimes in the night it would overwhelm her, and she would wonder how it was possible that, having lain in the same bed for forty years, she could not remember what it had felt like. Then she would think of their wedding day, those matte photos, and of how she would never sit beside him when he was old and sick, and yet she wanted to. She had always thought that regret was the price you paid for making a mistake, but every cell in her body told her that she had not.

Her face was becoming numb from the cold now and she pulled her jumper up over her mouth. As she walked, she could see Berllan-Deg coming back into view and, suddenly, she remembered the old tin tea caddy that Hannah and she had hidden in the orchard wall in order to pass messages to friends. The other children would run from the village and leave notes there, and she and Hannah would answer. She smiled and wondered if it was still there, looking for the loose stone which hid it. At first, it had been something that Hannah and Sadie had done together; then, as Hannah grew older, it had been for Sadie's use only. And her stomach began to tighten as she thought of her friend, the letters they used to leave there for each other, Sadie stealing paper to write on. Letters overblown and ridiculous, to make each other feel things they had never felt before. Testing, writing it down, because they could not talk openly, even to each other.

Sadie walked back along the hedgerow now; she was sure it had been around halfway along, behind a square stone. She pushed and pressed a few until she heard a metallic scrape. She smiled, her heart leaping – it was there! She pressed her fingers down the sides of the stone and pulled it out. A tin, rusted, the imagery smudged through with a rusty orange bloom. She pulled at the lid and it came away. The tin was empty, of course; she had known it would be. The last letter she had left there for her friend had never been collected, as she had moved away. Heartbroken, Sadie had taken it back, in case anyone came across it, and had thrown it into the fire.

'Sadie?'

Sadie spun around to see Megan watching her.

'I'm sorry, I didn't mean to . . .'

'It's OK.' Sadie exhaled. She looked down at the tin in her hands. 'I was just . . . We used this . . . it was just a way of passing messages to friends when we were young. Secrets. Unspoken things.' Sadie smiled and pushed the tin back into place, covering it with the stone. 'I was just wondering if it was still here.'

Sadie brushed off her hands.

'I think the thaw is coming,' said Megan, watching her.

'At least you can go home, then?'

Megan shrugged. 'Yes, I suppose so.'

'You don't sound terribly happy about it?'

Megan was laughing now. Sadie looked at her and realized her own smile was fading.

'I suppose, the snow, coming here . . . You know, I don't think I've ever stopped before.' Megan curled her fingers under the cuffs of her coat to keep them warm. There was a pinkness to the skin of her face.

'I know what that's like,' replied Sadie.

'I did well at school, so I started to do more and more, wanted to prove myself to someone, anyone . . .' She paused. 'It was something to tell my mother about when I called her. I was the first to go to college . . . These past weeks . . .' Megan shrugged again and Sadie was sure there were tears in her eyes. 'I think it's the quiet; it exposes you.'

Sadie tucked her hands into her pockets.

'Why do you think I talk so much?'

Megan smiled at her warmly.

'You'll figure things out, I'm sure.'

'I hope so,' Megan replied, her breath clouding in the air. 'Anyway, I'd better get back.'

Sadie nodded, watched as the dusk closed in around her as she walked away.

24

HANNAH HAD DREAMT OF the trees again; she had dreamt that she could hear them beginning to stir, the sap rising, turning outwards. She had dreamt that their roots had started growing towards the house and unsettled the foundations. She had been startled awake and then, lying in the darkness, she had thought of the way her father had planned out the orchard, his living memory, and a strange sadness had fallen upon her. She had got up early and listened, in the thin light downstairs, as the whole world around Berllan-Deg began to run with water. After what seemed like an eternity of stillness, there was movement. Dynamism. The orchard seemed to have a direction, a flow. The roads would be clear today. Hannah had drunk her tea by the fire and walked back and forth to the window while Sadie sat reading, raising her eyes occasionally.

She had then gone to the parlour, steeling herself against the memories within, and opened the old bureau by the fireplace where her father had kept the orchard papers. As dawn broke, she had sat in the kitchen reading her father's scrawling hand. The diagrams, the plans he had made, every tree's genus, its characteristics. There were weights and measures, invoices and receipts for glass cider bottles and repairs. Although Hannah had learnt everything from him, he had prevented her from making any decisions, from shaping the orchard in any way, from leaving her mark. She leafed through an old ledger which had been filled in sideways so that the trees' lineages could be traced across two pages. Let her tongue feel the names of the trees. There were ten-year diaries, too – each day marked with the weather, the price of animal feed, in October the bushels of apples harvested – and a few old books, the covers laden with images of Edens, of heavenly places gilded with golden apples. It was all hers now, but she felt no ownership over it.

She looked out at the black trees, stripped and naked in the thaw. She had already removed the dead wood, let the light in, but there was so much more work to do: the sward under the trees was matted and thick, and she would have to take away some of the trees that had suffocated and plant new ones where they stood. She would have to graft the old trees on to new rootstocks, and it was at this time of year that it was done. It would take years, of course, but looking out at the thaw she felt something stir inside her. She had felt numb since John's death, since Megan's arrival, she had felt subject to things that she could not change, but as she began to think of how the orchard could look, she knew that she alone had the knowledge to achieve it. There was a dim light in the canopy now and Hannah watched it grow through the dawn.

The roads would be clear today; Megan would be able to leave. She had walked towards the village the previous day and found enough reception to listen to her messages, including the frantic ones from the museum. Such messages would usually have stirred her into a panic, but she had felt strangely detached. Today she had got up early, made some tea, and had sat as usual on the caravan step and fed the birds. She had packed her clean clothes and thought of the way that she had been perfectly content with such a small selection here. She'd folded the heavy coat that Sadie had given her, too, and laid it on the bed. Lastly, she had written Jack a note, thanking him for letting her use the caravan, saying how it had been nice to meet him and asking him to write to let her know if the hives had survived the winter. She wasn't sure why, but she wanted to know. She cleaned out and re-laid the fire, so it was exactly as she had found it, then slung her bag over her shoulder and followed the path to the house. She knocked and Sadie answered.

Hannah and Sadie were eating breakfast, the table covered in papers and old books. Megan walked in, stood by the table a moment.

'I just wanted to say goodbye,' she said.

Hannah got to her feet, walked over to the dresser and opened a drawer there. She took out an old photograph, a grainy image from the eighties. A book signing, a man in a smart shirt, sideburns. She held it out to Megan, who took the picture, looked at it, and exhaled slowly. She could see her eyes, her own eyes. She glanced at Hannah – how difficult it must have been for her to see those eyes again.

'Thank you,' she said quietly as Hannah nodded. Then Megan remembered, reached into her pocket and pulled out the key that she had found in the orchard.

'I found this,' she said. 'I'm sorry to have intruded.'

'We asked you to come . . .' began Sadie.

'That's not what I meant,' said Megan softly, looking at Hannah. 'Thank you.'

Like the orchard, they stood in a triangle now, each one a corner. Then Megan turned to leave. She walked towards the door while Hannah stood staring at the key on the pear-wood table. Megan raised her hand to the door handle . . .

'Stop.' It was Hannah. Megan turned to face them.

'You don't have to go, that is . . . if you don't want to.'

Megan's face softened.

Sadie had been right: she did look unhappy. Lonely.

'You could stay for a while, until Jack comes back or . . .'

'Why?' Megan asked, her eyes filling with tears. 'Why would I?'

'I don't know,' said Hannah. 'Because you . . . part of you belongs here.'

Megan could not speak. Sadie smiled and Hannah turned away to make more tea.

'Well, that's that settled, then,' Hannah said under her breath, leaving Megan speechless by the door, the grainy image of her father still in her hand.

25

Work

*When the bees are a week to ten days old, they leave
the hive for the first time. Until now, they have felt
their way around their world, but on leaving the hive,
the realization dawns that they have been living in
darkness. Their joy is palpable on learning that the
walls of their world are infinite; they fly in circles,
upwards, downwards, expending energy in a way that
they never will again. For, once they have viewed the
world and mapped their home as an indelible mark
in their minds, their thoughts turn to work.*

*I have moved hives before now, have taken them
to the uplands for heather honey, have had to remove
and repair them, but so strong is the bees' sense of
home that if you place a hive even a foot from its
original position, then they will not find it. They
will die. So honed and precise is their feeling for
where they come from. However, if you move a hive
three miles or more, they find it with ease. It is as if
they recalibrate their entire worldview, and re-centre
themselves again.*

*When your entire world has changed, you see
things clearly for the first time; it is as if you live a
different life. However hard I tried, the world would
not let me see the life we had. Part of me died that
day, when the letter came to say she had been born.
I couldn't grieve for the birth of a child; that would*

*have been ridiculous, as you and I both know, more
than anyone, how much of a miracle a child can be, a
life is. It was more that I had not had this child with
you. Our home had shifted, and I felt lost outside it.*

*There are so many things that soothe a hive,
Hannah – good weather, nectar flow – but nothing
soothes the bees more than work. Over the years I
have noticed that it is one of the things they need most.
They need a purpose, an occupation, stimulation. You
can hear it in the hive when they have run out of room
to work. They will leave. If their work is disrupted by
rain, by thunder, if their queen is dead, they lose focus;
but if all is well, and they are working and the work
is going well, there is no greater sense of calm, for they
do not work for themselves, they work for others, for
the common good.*

*I have opened a hive at midday in midsummer
with no gloves, no veil. Bees that are occupied and
content are at ease, and they have choices – that is the
thing that most people do not realize. They can guard
the entrance, they can be architects, mathematicians,
geographers; they can collect pollen, nectar; they can
nurture the young or fight the enemy. They can be
handmaidens or undertakers – the only thing they
need is to find a passion for something, and with that
they can exist within life. Without it, they perish.*

*So, I turned to my books, Hannah. I suppose they
gave me purpose. It felt good to conserve the Welsh
language, to hold on to something that sometimes
feels as if it is slipping away. To feel its beauty
and record it, to know that language comes from*

landscape, to find different words rooted just twenty miles apart. To see the world through letters. The thought crosses my mind, occasionally, that my books will be looked at in the far future as curiosities, a record of a language long gone, but I have worked to show the value it holds, the traditions it cherishes, and that must mean something?

Work can be difficult, Hannah. Many times, I have watched bees try to draw pollen and nectar from reluctant flowers. If it has been dry, the nectar is thicker, more viscous, but sometimes, around mid-June, you will see a change. There are rivers, in the fields, of nectar. We cannot see them, but they are there, and sometimes a bee will arrive back at the hive heralding with a dance that it has found one and the bees may steal its waters. The work becomes easy, and the rewards abundant. I only wish that sometimes they stopped. I only wish that sometimes I had stopped, to see what was in front of me. Two years, three, on one book, and then another, and a decade or two would slip by. It was my occupation, my preoccupation, the place where I hid, and I know you came to find me there, in the way you'd sit and listen to me talking about the latest book. The changes you'd suggest, the infuriating way you always seemed to be able to get to the heart of any weakness in the work. Your father made it impossible for you to be in the orchard; he shut you out of something that was part of you. We all shut you out from being a mother. I shut you out with my books; I made up stories and left our own neglected.

26

THE ROOTSTOCKS THAT HANNAH had ordered had
been left in a crate by the side of the lane. Hannah
collected them and carried them back to the shed
through the orchard. Snowdrops had sliced through
the sward and were now carpeting the orchard floor.
Hannah had never seen so many; it was as if the snow
had shocked them into imitation. She placed the crate
on a bench and went to the shed in search of her father's
knives, which she found on a ledge, their blades dull.
She rummaged in a box of tools for the grinding stone
and circled her chosen blade carefully across its dull
surface, raising a grey dust which hung in the air.

She had collected the scion wood from the trees
the day before, had looked for sections with buds and
cut them, wrapped them in a piece of cloth, and put
them on the bench in the shed. Today she would have
to cut both the rootstock and the scion wood and bind
them together so that they would grow as one. She
tested the blade with her thumb and felt it catch her
skin. It was sharp enough. Then she carried the knife
to the house.

Sadie had been eating breakfast at the table and
tried not to show too much interest as Hannah walked
in, not taking off her boots before sterilizing the knife in
some boiling water. When she went back out, Sadie
followed her. She leant on the doorframe of the shed
as Hannah examined each scion and each rootstock

before making a diagonal cut into both, measuring by eye the notch needed, the tongue which would latch the two pieces of wood together. It was strange when you were grafting, but it was the thin green layer of wood on the outside that needed to be matched, not the heartwood. That would eventually fuse together; it was the more superficial layer that made the difference to the graft taking or failing. Hannah pushed the two woods together, making sure that there was a small white notch visible, the church window, which would encourage the callus to take hold.

Hannah repeated the process over and over, cutting and wounding and shaping and then bandaging the cuts tightly to encourage them to take. Afterwards, she motioned to Sadie to help her, and they carried bundles of grafted rootstock out into the orchard. Then the two of them spent the rest of the day planting them, temporarily, so that they had time to strengthen before being moved to their growing positions. Sadie had not seen Hannah so focused in a long time; there was a new energy about her. When they finished, they straightened their aching backs, observing the whip-thin trees in rows by the hedge. They would not know if they had taken for five to six weeks, by which time, if everything worked, the buds on the scion wood would start to swell, a sign that the two woods were now acting as one. There had been no new trees in Berllan-Deg for years. Hannah would use some of the varieties that were already there through this grafting, but she would also order some new trees that she realized she had been wanting to grow for years. It was getting late, and Hannah noticed that it was a little lighter than it had been. There were no sure signs of spring yet, but it must be on its way.

Megan had begun to eat with them in the house; it seemed to make more sense than Sadie having to carry plates back and forth. The table was now permanently covered in paperwork and plans, and Megan would smile at Sadie about Hannah's new project. Hannah would get up distractedly after every meal and go to sit at her father's bureau in the parlour, and Sadie and Megan would remain together, Sadie feeling safe to leave more silences between them now as she got to know Megan a little better.

'So what did the museum have to say about you not going back?' Sadie asked.

Megan sighed. 'They weren't too happy,' she replied.

'I can imagine,' smiled Sadie.

'In fact, I'm no longer employed there,' admitted Megan.

'And how do you feel about that?'

Megan frowned. 'The girl I share a flat with has found someone to take my room; the museum was looking to make cuts in staff anyway. What kind of life did I have that I could slip out of it so easily? So seamlessly?' she asked.

Megan fell silent but could see that Sadie's eyes were glistening with tears.

'Are you married?' asked Megan eventually.

'I was.' Sadie composed herself, cleared her throat. 'I left him. A few years ago. We didn't have any children.'

Megan nodded. 'I had a boyfriend when I was really young. We grew up together. I think . . . maybe things at home . . . I was looking for stability or something. We were dependent on each other.' She paused a moment. 'There's been no one since.'

'Can I ask a favour?' she asked after a while.

'Of course.'

'Can I borrow a few books? It's just there aren't many in the caravan, and coming back here . . .' She shrugged. 'I've not read any Welsh for years and I could do with a little distraction.'

Sadie paused. 'Come with me.'

Megan's eyes widened as she scanned the shelves in John's office.

'I'm afraid they're a bit jumbled up,' Sadie said.

'There are so many!'

Sadie gave her a tight smile. 'Well, it was his life,' she murmured. She watched as Megan began to leaf through the titles.

Megan somehow felt a deep relief at seeing all the books, a few she was familiar with; they gave her a sense of being at home. She looked over at Sadie and smiled.

'I'll leave you to it, then,' Sadie said, walking past her. 'Take as many as you want.'

Megan looked back at the shelves. Each one was overfull, books stacked on top of each other to the extent that the wooden slats bowed a little under their weight.

27

WEEKS HAD PASSED. MEGAN had taken a lot of the books off the shelves, placed them on John's desk and instinctively started to recategorize them. She had never had much space to keep books of her own; most of hers had been borrowed from the library or bought from and taken back to second-hand bookshops on a one-in-one-out basis. There was a plethora of nature books, on shells and algae, sea tides and wildflowers, along with around twenty books on birdwatching. Then there were plays and poetry, a huge number of reference books, and, on the highest shelves, rows and rows of novels – classics mostly, but also some contemporary writers in Welsh and English. Megan had spent the days opening them, trying to see what the books had in common, where her father's interests had lain. There was an incongruency to some of his choices, too: religious books and atheist texts, books on folklore and books on scientific theories. She had concluded that some must have been for research, a reflection of a curious mind.

She was sitting in the caravan now, leafing through a book on wildflowers, when she heard a gentle knock.

'Come in?'

It was Sadie, some books in her hands, a certain tentativeness about her. Megan held the door open.

'I don't know if you'd be interested in these? They were some of the books your father wrote.'

'He actually published?'

'They're technical books mostly. He worked on a dictionary, some phrase books; he specialized in dialects.'

'So he was a conservationist in some ways?'

'I suppose so, a bit like you,' agreed Sadie.

'I've just made some coffee,' said Megan, 'if you want some?'

Sadie came in, noticing that it was homelier in the van than when Jack was there, the fire lit. Megan placed the books on the shelf behind the bed, trying not to look at them until Sadie had gone, every inch of her wanting to devour them.

'I've been trying to look for him in his collection,' Megan admitted, 'to find out about his interests and so on. Perhaps it's a force of habit.'

'And what do you think?'

Megan shrugged. 'He's . . . intriguing.'

'If it's any consolation, I don't think I knew him very well, either.'

Megan looked surprised by this.

'I thought I did. I was so certain. The older I get, the less I seem to know.' Sadie took a sip of coffee. 'He was very talented, funny, sociable when it suited him, but he also had another side.' Sadie felt her voice change. 'He could be quiet, scathing about himself and other people.'

Megan considered this. 'I thought that if I knew more about him, it might help me . . . I don't know . . . piece myself together a little better. Does that make sense?'

'Of course.'

'It's just that sometimes I feel so scattered, so anxious. It's been a little better since I came here, but . . .' She shrugged. 'Have you ever felt like that?'

Sadie felt her stomach knot. 'I have,' she said, breathing out, a stifled tension released. 'In fact, I had a breakdown.'

Megan's eyes softened.

'Before I was thirty, not much older than you are now. I never told anyone except my then husband.'

Megan could sense the fragility of the moment, knew not to say anything.

'I suppose we didn't talk about things like that then. They used to put everything down to "women's problems" . . . It started suddenly one day, this deep-seated feeling that something was wrong. Then it escalated; I made mistakes at work, I couldn't sleep. I would have these thoughts, thoughts I never dreamt I would have had.'

The fire crackled in the momentary silence.

'The worst thing was that there was nowhere I could feel safe, and when these thoughts came, I didn't even feel safe with myself.'

There were tears on Megan's face now.

'I can understand that,' she said.

'I suppose that's what we all want, isn't it?' said Sadie, drawing a deep breath. 'A place to feel safe?'

28

THE CROCUSES FLAMED THROUGH the orchard in blackbird-beak orange, a tenuous warmth building in the air. The catkins were dusted with yellow pollen and the hazel around the orchard had regrouped, buds strung like beads along its limbs. Today, the sky was a cornflower blue, and the breeze felt newly washed. Hannah looked over at the blackthorn, its wretched gnarled form covered in delicate white flowers. She hung the sheets on the line; she had noticed that the sky had been a pinkish purple the night before, guessed that they might have a fine day, and had stripped all the beds.

It had taken a few weeks, but now they had settled into a fragile new rhythm: Sadie and Hannah in the house, Megan in the caravan but coming in more, sitting and reading in silence with Sadie, following Hannah around the orchard. She had ventured further, too, into the village, and had bought herself a bicycle.

Hannah pegged the last of the sheets on the line, and watched as the breeze blew through them. She had spent the last few weeks working in the orchard, removing lichen where it had grown too thickly, refining the work on some of the trees. That would have to stop now as the sap was rising. Every night, she would fall into a dreamless sleep, after which she would wake early and drink her tea, looking once more at the plans she had made for the orchard.

She saw Megan come out of the caravan and give her a wave. Hannah nodded back and watched as the younger woman got on her bike and pedalled away. Hannah picked up the basket and walked back into the house. This morning, she had some work to do, so, for the first time in a long time, she walked into the office, noticing as she did that Megan had reorganized John's books. They were not exactly as Hannah remembered them, but Megan had put everything back on the shelves immaculately and there was a sense to the way she had done it, a purpose.

Hannah sat at John's desk and started researching the apples she wanted to plant, made phone enquiries and ordered some new trees. She would be just in time to plant them. She wanted more eating apples, which would be sweeter and less tart than the cider varieties. She chose old, endangered types, varieties that might not be as vigorous as the ones her father had grown, that needed time and patience and a knowledgeable arborist. Many of them had been sidelined over the years, as they were found to be less easy to establish, or they did not bear enough fruit, or they didn't fruit quickly or reliably enough. Hannah became lost in images of apples of every colour – extremely small and almost purple, some round and blushing like children's cheeks, some elongated with a square shape, and some whose blood-red colouring seeped into the white flesh, making it look stained. She had even found the enlli apple, rescued from the coast and said to have been the one eaten by Eve herself. The new trees would arrive soon. She had marked them all in her father's notebook – the males and females, ones which pollinated themselves, the ones pollinated by wind and the ones that needed the bees – and she felt her anticipation growing. Recently, she had felt a little stronger, too; perhaps it was the time she had been spending outside, or the way her mind was working on the orchard.

Sadie had become increasingly preoccupied since she had told Megan about her breakdown. She had been thinking back over that time, the way her mind had blanked out some of the details. Perhaps it was the medication, or perhaps it had been her own mind protecting her present self from her past self, but what had been most difficult was Seth's kindness, his support, the way that he had stayed with her from start to finish. She had felt caught between her guilt and her need to forgive herself for the fact that she would never be everything he needed; she had also needed to forgive him for the fact that he would never be what she needed. She had stayed with him then, absorbing the evidence that he was a good man, a good friend. They were getting older and the physical side of their relationship would eventually wind down anyway, and, in this way, they had lived happily until the insomnia had begun again, around six years ago. Despite her talking it down, her body would not let her rest, would not allow her to settle.

And then she had met Anne, and everything had fallen apart. She would not talk to her, would not go near her, as the volatility of what she felt around her was frightening. She would go home, make the dinner, read the paper and talk to Seth about what she'd done at work that day. And then she would berate herself that the world had changed – that she was an old woman, a grown woman, and this shouldn't be so difficult. Giving herself permission should not be so difficult. Yet still there was something in her that told her it would be easier to stay with Seth. Something that had been seeded in her, something about the comfort of others.

Eventually, she had to tell Seth that she did not love him any more and witness his bewilderment, the way she had taken his life out from under him just as he was looking forward to retiring. She remembered his pleading, asking why, and she had not been able to enunciate it, because she had not known for sure herself. She'd had to shrug her shoulders, lie, the titters that had haunted her childhood ringing in her ears, the hushed tones and the fear that her friends would know who she was.

And then she had lived alone, ignoring the quizzical looks of her friends, consolidating herself, and suddenly she had become aware of the privileges that came with being married, and their loss. Not the monetary ones but the social ones, the protection that it afforded. Invitations that circled around Seth, a certain tension in friends' questions, a deep-rooted fear that such a long marriage could seemingly fall apart with no explanation; the way none of them had predicted it. And then she had seen Anne again, who had asked her to go walking with her, and Sadie had felt compelled to do so even though she was not as fit as she had been. The ease and fluidity of their conversation had shocked Sadie, the way they had discussed the end of Sadie's marriage without discussing why, their unspoken understanding. The silence as they stood on the tops of hills and the smallness of everything below. She had felt herself grow.

This morning, when she had woken to the bright, unforgiving spring light, she had not turned away from it. She had started to gather her things, clear up her old room, pulling down the sheets. Anne had told her to take her time to think, but what Sadie had begun to realize was that time was not on their side. She stuffed her things into a bag and walked down the stairs.

'Hannah?'

She could not see her.

'Yes?'

Sadie followed Hannah's voice through to the office. Her sister was sitting at John's desk, a place Sadie had never seen her sit before.

'I need to go home for a while,' she said.

Hannah put down the book she was holding.

'Is everything all right?'

'Of course. I just . . . I need to see someone. I won't be long.'

Hannah nodded.

'I don't want you to worry.' Sadie smiled.

Hannah watched as she disappeared through the door. She listened as her familiar footsteps receded and waited to hear her car engine start before getting up and walking to the window that looked out on to the lane.

Megan had spent the morning riding her bicycle around the lanes, the once bewildering network now second nature. She had stopped to see two hares fighting in the middle of a ploughed field and then made her way back, pedalling faster and faster.

She had been listening more to the birds, had spent time reading, and for the first time in years she found her anxiety beginning to lessen. She had begun to get up with the light instead of according to some timetable; she would read until she was tired, eat when she was hungry, and discovered that she had seasons within, intuitions that had been trying to whisper to her. Over the years she had become so adept at ignoring the ways her body tried to talk to her, of disregarding her own discomfort, that she had become used to headaches and a churning stomach and neck muscles that ached from morning to night. She had some savings left, and she didn't spend much here, so the question was more what she should do next, where to go.

She cycled down the lane and saw Berllan-Deg in the distance; with one hand she unbuttoned her coat so that it flew out behind her. She could not stay here for ever, she knew that, but she needed to rest awhile. She felt the surprising warmth of the breeze on her face as she freewheeled next to the hedge and then pressed the brakes, and that was when she saw them: bees on the catkins. Only one, then two lone bees. She stopped, her face flushed from cycling, then she pushed her bike into the orchard, leant it against the caravan and walked towards the hives. She turned her head, listening and listening. The blackbirds were in full song today, the chiffchaffs too, but there was something else. An undertone. She approached the hives, trying to control her breathing. There didn't seem to be any movement there. Puzzled, she walked nearer. There was a lot of what looked like dirt at the entrance to the first hive. She listened again, and then she saw them. One, two bees leaving the hive, launching themselves upwards, their flight path straight from the doorway towards the hazel hedging. Megan's heart leapt, her eyes bewitched, so much so that she didn't hear Jack walking up behind her.

'So, they're alive, then.'

Megan swung around, startled.

'Yes,' she said, beaming. 'They're alive!'

29

Language

*People will speak of the language of bees; you will
have heard them, Hannah, mimicking the hum, but
the bees' language is more sophisticated than that.
They are, in fact, beyond language; they communicate
in ways that we can only dream of. I have often
envied them that ability, the way they embody their
message physically and chemically. Their business
is scent, pheromones, perfume. They are constantly
in communication, leaving trails wherever they go,
reading each other's wishes in the ether. Can you
imagine if we could understand each other like that?
If we could silently tell people of our needs?*

*Our words, Hannah, are clumsy, blunt, noisy; we
lack the sophistication of the bees, the intensity of the
contact they keep. We are animals, while they seem
divine.*

*There is an exquisite sensitivity that radiates from
them. I have told you many times that the smell of
sweat infuriates them, synthetic perfumes too. Can
you imagine the onslaught those must be for them?
Imagine you could taste the air, breathe someone
in, and that your senses were raw, so incredibly
sublime. I sometimes wonder why they tolerate
us. The bumbling way we open a hive even after
half a century of practice, our noisy breathing, our
abrasiveness.*

That is one of our greatest failures, Hannah.
We used to speak constantly, the way you occupied
my mind, the way I occupied yours, the way we
constantly looked at each other, not just in affection,
but in reassurance. You were well, I was well, and all
was well; then, as we became older, the words seemed
to quieten, and we learnt to speak without speaking,
to notice and ignore, to exist side by side. I fell for
the silence, Hannah. I let it be that way, yet I had
so much to tell you. We do not have the ability to be
silent like the bees; we do not have their talent, their
clarity; we cannot reach inside another's mind, and
that is what has frustrated me tonight. I could get up
now, reach for my walking stick, and come and wake
you. I could sit on our bed, the one we have lain in
for so many years, and begin to try to explain, if I had
another lifetime. But what use would it be?

    This has been our life, but if I could live it over
again, I would have done my best to look to you, to
read you, to bring my mind closer to yours; I would
have tried to notice the signs. I did not have the bees'
finesse and I am afraid that my words, our words,
will never have it. That is our tragedy. We cannot feel
what it is to fully understand the people around us,
to change course symbiotically, to predict each other's
needs. To know them in every sense, in our bodies and
minds and in the air around us. The space between
us will always exist, the space between us which is
silence, and reticence, and ink on paper. That paper-
thin distance.

    So, tonight, I will find my stick and walk to the

kitchen, look around at the home we have made together, and I will climb the stairs to you as I have done for so many decades, and I will undress and lie next to you as you sleep on your side, and I will lay my hand on your hip and wait there until my breathing deepens into sleep. I will wonder about the fragrances I have known, the warm spicy scent of the propolis in a beehive on a summer's day, the leather belt my father beat me with, the rubber on the wheels of my first car, the lily of the valley on our wedding day, the sweet smell of your breath on our wedding night. Your scent on my jumpers, the wax polish that I made for you for the table, the blossom in the orchard, the soil here the morning after heavy rain, the scent of books. Perhaps it is in this way that the bees see me; perhaps to them I am nothing more than these moments in the ether. I don't know if you will remember me sometimes, when I am gone. Perhaps it will be the scent of me in an old coat or a scarf, and I hope that it will not hurt you, that instead it will remind you of the time that we have had together. It seems impossible now, that I will be gone, but perhaps that is just our lack of understanding, our stupidity, our limitation.

I think the bees knew, the last time I tended to them. It was midsummer, and when I opened the hive, they were quiet. As I took out each frame, some of them climbed on to my hands, gentle, tolerant. The queen was laying well, they were in a nectar flow, they were working, but for a moment they stopped and seemed to acknowledge me before carrying on.

Their desire is to live, to thrive, and I hope that is what you will do. I hope that you can forgive me, even though I am deserving of your contempt and your anger. Don't stop, Hannah, although I have no right to tell you that, but don't stop. There is a life in you that words cannot hold.

30

JACK OPENED THE HIVES without smoke. The bees would not be very active yet, still drowsy from their cluster, so he did not fear they would attack him. The crown board was stuck fast, as they had glued it shut with propolis to keep draughts out. He pushed the hive tool under it, and heard it crack as he lifted it. There was no honey super there at this time of year, only the nest and a super for their winter stores. No queen excluder to keep the queen from laying in the honey. Jack's gladness at seeing a few bees outside the hive was always tempered at this time of year, as their survival was precarious, depending on the weather and whether the queen had once again begun laying.

He pulled out the outer frame and leant it against the hive to make some room, trying to ignore the concern in the pit of his stomach. The cluster had loosened; they seemed to be tentatively beginning to work. He did not want to disturb them too much, so he pulled the frames across and tried to pinch out a frame close to the middle; he needed to work quickly so he didn't let the nest get too cold. He hitched out the frame and held it to the spring light, angled it towards the sun so he could see. There were only a few brood cells, domed and mustard-coloured, a few thin cells of pollen clustered together as an artist might organize a palette, but it was difficult to see. The eggs would be laid by the queen in curves; John had brought that to his attention, the way she would place each one centrally in the cells, each one a minute comma, an anticipation of what would come next. He could not see any and, concerned, he replaced the frame. He moved closer to the middle of the nest, prising another frame from its position; the bees were active but not frantic, a gradual turning back towards the world.

John had shown him what to look for, how to read the frames, and Jack had surprised himself with the way he had enjoyed learning. At school, he had found that books, words, frustrated him, but this he had an intuition for, looking at the patternation of pollen, the domed cells, the ratio of nectar to pollen, the number of brood and eggs, the delicate balance required for a healthy hive. John had also envied the way Jack could always find the queen. He would say that some had a knack for it, while others would rarely see her and had to be content to look at the evidence that she was or had been there recently. Each queen would be marked with a coloured dot to denote which year she had been born; in this way, the beekeeper could know how old she was and when she was likely to be replaced, although that had recently been brought into question.

John had told him about the halcyon days of bee-keeping, the days when colonies thrived, when stores were full and queens would live for three years, sometimes more, which was extraordinary considering that the average worker lived for just six weeks in summer. Things were different now. The weather was changing, becoming unpredictable, the landscape was more hostile, and queens would sometimes stop laying, or would die after only six months for no discernible reason.

Colonies would collapse, viruses would take hold, and it had been clear for some time that the queens were not happy, that the environment was difficult for them. Old queens were a rarity, the young ones unsettled. Jack had inherited troubles from the beekeepers who had come before him, and he had to find new solutions.

He held the new frame up to the light again and squinted. He had to monitor the bees more now, feed them, keep them warm. He would check the number of eggs and would often find his heart sinking when he realized that the queen had died, or had left. He had seen hives starving in midsummer. It was hard to believe, but there would be a natural gap in June for two weeks, when the spring flowers had given their all and the summer ones had not yet matured, fourteen days of starvation in the middle of what seemed like abundance. If the bees had enough stores, they could survive, of course, but it wasn't unusual now to find a hive dwindling or dead just as summer got under way.

A few bees were circling his face, but they weren't aggressive, which led him to believe that the queen must be in there somewhere. He tried to soften his focus – he found that, sometimes, looking for the shape rather than the individual worked best, her almond elongated body, her amber colour. Then he saw them, the eggs, and felt his shoulders relax. They were there in curves, one after another; her work precise, immaculate. It had been the angle of the sun. He did not have to see the queen herself; she was obviously busy and seemed to be strong. Smiling, he was satisfied, and sought to close the hive as quickly as possible.

John had always kept three hives. There were so many challenges these days that owning one wasn't sufficient, and having three gave you the ability to fix problems. You could borrow some brood from one hive, or you could start a new colony by taking a queen cell from one hive and putting it in another. It was as if each hive relied increasingly on the colonies around it. Each fragile culture unable to survive alone, looking to the others for help. The second hive had eggs, the last one a few. Jack continued to assess them until he was happy that he had seen what he needed to see and understood what he needed to understand. Then, he pulled the veil up over his head and breathed in the spring air.

He would need to look at the hives again in a week or so, but he rested his hand on the roof of the nearest one and momentarily thought of John. The time he had given Jack, the way he had humoured his mistakes as he learnt how to manage things at the orchard. The way he had nurtured him, knowing, perhaps instinctively, that the boy had been a little bit lost. Jack had been laying a hazel hedge when he heard of his passing; someone had stopped to talk on the road and had given Jack his condolences. Jack had not shown that he hadn't heard the news, but when the person had driven away, he had gone to his fire and pushed the kettle on to the embers. He'd sat for a long time, thinking about John, about Hannah.

He rarely saw his own father now, had little desire to. When he was a boy, he could feel his father's frustration with him, over his school marks, his behaviour, and, as Jack grew into a man, his lack of ambition exasperated him. His father would come and visit and, despite his best efforts, there would be some bemusement as he watched Jack laying a hedge or putting in fencing. Their incompatibility stemmed from more than just his father's dismissiveness towards Jack's skills; it was more that they seemed to be fundamentally made from such different things, like different woods: his father like hazel – impatient, willing to change and take advantage of opportunities – and himself a little more slow-growing. The tension turned into a feigned indifference on Jack's side, and a barely concealed contempt on his father's.

He had thought about finishing laying the hedge on the day that John died, but he could not. He had sat looking at the fire until it had grown dark. He brought to mind the last time they had seen each other: John had been sitting inside and Jack had updated him on the bees' progress. He had taken a full frame of honey to him, and they had shared some tea. Hannah with a hand on John's shoulder, John slicing the honeycomb – wax and all – into small squares to eat with bread and butter. Jack was satisfied with that; he could find peace in that. He would not go to the funeral, not because he did not care for John, but because he did not care for funerals. It was well known around here: if you wanted to be loved and praised by the people around you, the most effective thing you could do was die. Jack could not stomach the cloyingness of these occasions, the faux seriousness before the drinking of more tea and the eating of cake.

A slight vibration under his hand brought him back to the present. He had been worried about the hives, had taken more care than usual this winter, and everything seemed to have gone in his and the hives' favour, and he felt a great relief in that. He looked across the orchard towards Berllan-Deg. They would need good weather now, no sudden coldness – what they needed was stability.

31

MEGAN'S EXCITEMENT AT SEEING the bees had quickly dissipated into guilty disappointment at Jack's return. As glad as she was to see him, she knew it meant that her time in the caravan and Berllan-Deg was over. She had exchanged pleasantries with Jack and walked back to the caravan to pack. It was warmer inside today, the spring sun magnified through the windows, the light showing up all the dust and dirt, but she had grown to love the place anyway. Its sounds – not just of the birds, but the creak of the van in strong winds, the sound of rain on its roof – its ramshackle shelves, and the sometimes infuriating stove which had seemed to have a life of its own before she learnt how to light it properly.

She stripped the bed, placing the sheet inside the pillowcase to take to the house for washing. Then she began collecting up her clothes. She would only wear a few items, even after being sent more by her flatmate. The clothes she had worn before did not suit who and where she was now, and she had even 'borrowed' one of Jack's jumpers on a particularly cold night. As she looked at her things, she realized they felt alien to her, that they somehow belonged to another world. She packed everything up as small as she could and stuffed it into a rucksack. Then she picked up the clock that she had been sent, the one she had quickly taken the battery out of and laid face down on the side table as its ticking had irritated her. She stuffed it reluctantly into her bag along with the hairbrush she barely used. Since there was no way to dry her hair here, except to sit in front of the fire, it had reverted to a wavy texture that she did not want to pull at with a comb or a brush.

She would have to take back John's books, too, the latest ones she had borrowed from his office. That pained her also – the thought that she had begun to get a sense of him, to find his shape in the space he had left in Hannah's, Sadie's and Jack's lives.

She began to take down the books and put them in piles.

'You leaving us?' She had not noticed Hannah at the door, watching her.

Startled, Megan placed her hand on her chest, then smiled.

'Come in,' she said.

Hannah shook her head.

Megan waited for Hannah to say something.

'I just wanted to say that Sadie has gone home for a little while.'

Megan could see that there was a certain seriousness in Hannah's face.

'Oh,' she said, slightly crestfallen. 'She didn't say goodbye.'

'It was a bit sudden,' answered Hannah.

Megan nodded. 'I'll go home, too, I suppose, now that Jack's back. Think about what to do next . . .'

'I was just going to clean up Sadie's room,' Hannah said, and Megan wondered why she'd come to say this to her until she finally understood the game she was in.

She thought a moment, her heart racing, not wanting to let anything show on her face.

'It won't take me too long,' said Hannah.

'Well, if the room is going to be empty,' suggested Megan, 'it *might* be a shame to keep it warm for nothing. And I could maybe help a bit around the place?'

Hannah's face softened.

'Well, do as you please. I was just telling you.'

Hannah turned abruptly and retreated through the orchard, and Megan watched her go, a slow smile spreading across her face.

Jack had called in to see his mother. She had taken a long time to organize the tea, flustered at his sudden arrival and having to find cups and plates for two. Jack had watched her, noticing that she looked much older than she had a year ago. She had retired now from being a cook at the local school and was finding it difficult to differentiate between the days, not having found a new routine yet. He had sat with her a long time, fixed a cupboard in the kitchen, and then kissed her cheek as he left.

He felt himself warming up as he walked, his mind still on how suddenly age had come to his mother. His father had needled him about the precariousness of Jack's situation, his lifestyle; said that he had known others like Jack and witnessed the brutality of his kind of life when you became old. The cold that would penetrate older bones, the aches, the relentless physicality of it. How irresponsible his lifestyle was and that he could not expect anyone else to live as he did. Jack had swallowed down his indignation but could not shrug off the feeling that his father was somehow right, and somewhere deep inside himself he had heard a door close.

Jack knew these lanes by instinct. He had run in them as a child, sledged through them when it had snowed, and found his way home in the darkness when he had started drinking. On pitch-black nights when he could not see even a few feet in front of him, he would tip his head up and look at the sky between the trees above him and follow that. He would listen, too, count the streams towards Berllan-Deg, know how many he had to navigate. The days were lengthening now, and when the night came, it came more gradually, a certain milkiness to it.

He listened to his footsteps as Berllan-Deg came into view. There was a dim light across the orchard, smoke coming from the chimney. The house had looked the same ever since he was a child: the solid walls, the cornerstone by the door that seemed to be both part of the wall and part of the foundation, where John used to sit sometimes and wait for him to arrive in the mornings, a smile broadening on seeing him. The whole place was unchanged, yet everything had changed. He had seen it in nature, too, a long continuation shattered by a sudden event, decades of stability changed in a landslide, or the fall of a tree, or the bursting of a riverbank.

Jack moved through the gap in the hedge and walked towards the caravan. The bed had been stripped and the fire in the stove had been re-laid, ready to be lit. It had been John's idea: to buy the caravan and put it in the orchard so Jack could have his independence when he was young, and didn't have to travel back and forth between home and Berllan-Deg. As Jack grew, and was offered work elsewhere with the seasons, he had used it as a summer base. Sometimes he still stayed at home with his mother in bad weather or in winter, but every time he arrived here in spring, he experienced a peace he did not find anywhere else.

The caravan was his home, and his home had given him the freedom to go where he pleased, to take the work he wanted. Yet it was no directionless wanderlust, but a cyclical journey through the year that began and ended in autumn.

Jack pulled his sleeping bag out of its cover and laid it on the bed as he usually did. He took out some clothes and tossed them on the bench at the other side of the caravan. Although Megan had left and there was no discernible trace of her, the caravan felt different somehow, unfamiliar. He turned and looked around. There were some books that he presumed were John's, but not much else. He tried to pinpoint what it was for a moment, before thinking that perhaps it was her smell, her perfume in a place which had always smelt of wood and coffee and dampness. He smiled softly and reached for the matches to warm the place up.

32

'THE BEES ARE ALIVE,' said Megan as Hannah brought the food to the table. 'I thought you'd like to know.'

The kitchen was warm tonight, and Hannah had left the door open to let the breeze flow into the house. There were only the two of them.

'I'm glad,' Hannah said, betraying nothing on her face.

'Did you do anything with them? The bees, that is?'

Hannah shook her head. 'The bees were John's delight.'

Megan began eating, her appetite renewed by the thought of staying at Berllan-Deg a little longer. Hannah watched her, tried not to look at the way she held her fork, exactly as he had done. Her mind wandered to John, to the bees.

'They were his lifelong love, I think,' Hannah said truthfully. 'When we married, he started here, although he'd take some hives to the mountain sometimes, so we could gather heather honey.'

Megan added this to the growing imagery of her father she had in her head.

'I used to help him at the beginning.' Hannah smiled. 'I think I was trying to impress him.'

'Well,' replied Megan, raising her eyebrows, 'we've all done that kind of thing.'

Hannah continued, feeling him near somehow. 'I remember, once, I ordered him a new bee suit for his birthday. I ordered it from somewhere and he didn't check it, he took it out to use it, and it must have been cheap or something because in half an hour he was back in pain.'

Megan looked at her seriously.

'The pockets hadn't been sewn up, so he had trousers full of bees!'

Hannah's face creased unexpectedly and Megan laughed, too, shocked by Hannah's mirth. And as they laughed together, Hannah realized she had not laughed like that for a long time, her shoulders aching with it.

'Then there was the time he bought some bees from someone, when he was younger, and they told him the bees weren't very good-natured. Well, he thought he could cope with them . . .' Hannah rolled her eyes. 'My goodness, they stung him. They'd wait for him by the door, here – I've never known anything like it. They even stung him through his suit, on his face. And it wouldn't have mattered, but he was launching this book and had to speak in front of everyone . . .' Hannah's laughter was bubbling up now, her stomach starting to bounce with it, the words being jogged out of her. 'He had one eye fully closed, looked like he'd been in a ring with a boxer. There were pictures in the papers and everything!'

Megan giggled along with her.

'Serves him right,' Hannah concluded.

Eventually their laughter petered out, but a certain warmth between them remained.

'I was always more about the trees,' Hannah confided, her face flushed. 'But I never took the opportunity to make them my own. There was always something, someone to look after.' She put down her fork. 'My father used to tell me these stories – they were just stories, just silly . . .'

'What kind?' Megan leant in. Hannah searched her eyes a moment, wondering whether she should share them.

'He'd tell me how some people through history believed that Eden still existed, or that it had been scattered across the world, and these people had spent their lives trying to bring the pieces back together.'

Hannah recognized in Megan's eyes the same kind of rapture she had felt as she'd sat listening to her father.

'They're all just stories, of course,' she said dismissively, 'but I have been wondering lately what it would be like if you could begin your own Eden, on your own terms . . . to forget what you have inherited.'

Megan thought about it, the choices she would make, the strictures she had shed recently that she hadn't noticed were there before.

'If we could make our own orchard with what was important to us.'

'It sounds so simple, doesn't it?' said Megan quietly.

'It does,' agreed Hannah.

That evening Megan heard movement in the orchard outside. She got up and looked out of the window – it was Hannah, with something in her hand. Hannah approached a tree and seemed to be marking it. Megan frowned. Hannah was not what she had imagined her to be on that fraught journey here. There was a dignity to the older woman that had blindsided Megan. She had come prepared for confrontation, but she had not been met with it, not in the way she had expected. Perhaps it was her age, perhaps it was something to do with her stillness; Megan could not even imagine Hannah outside the orchard and she envied her. For belonging to a place so wholly.

Hannah was walking towards the furthest hedge now. Without thinking, Megan pulled on her boots and went outside, noticing as she did that there was a certain warmth in the air this evening, a certain fragrance that reminded her of spring. As she walked towards Hannah, she saw on the nearest tree a cross that Hannah had made on its ancient trunk. A mark in white chalk, luminous through the greying light.

'They'll need to be removed,' said Hannah, scratching a mark on another tree, a silent compassion in her eyes as she looked at its ageing crown. 'It has to be done. They were planted on a diagonal, can you see?'

For the first time, Megan realized there was a pattern of sorts, that the trees were planted in a kind of harlequin diamond grid.

'These ones are too far gone; they need to be taken out, the roots as well.'

'How long do they normally live?' asked Megan.

Hannah shrugged. 'My father planted some of them, the youngest ones – they can live eighty, sometimes a hundred years – but these, these are the oldest ones.'

Hannah's face seemed more open here, outside, away from the house and the low ceilings. She turned and began walking towards another tree, and Megan followed her.

'How do you know? When a tree won't come back in spring?' she asked.

'As they get older, their structure gets more complicated, so they think less about fruit. I suppose you could say they turn inwards.'

Megan nodded.

'It seems such a shame,' she said.

Hannah marked the tree, looked up at its twisted form.

'Yes,' she murmured.

Then, they continued the work in silence, each white cross a sign of a life drawing to its end.

33

JACK STARTED WORK EARLY. Hannah had shown him the crosses at first light and he had been considering the best way to remove the trees. Although they were old, their trunks weren't too thick, but Jack knew how vast their roots would be. He had seen them before in orchards, one tree's roots reaching another's so they could communicate. Felling one would affect all the others and he wanted to do it without shocking them. He had seen old men chopping down trees, then soaking the stumps in petrol to burn them, but he had always found that undignified somehow. He had decided that the kindest way would be to fell them then dig the roots out by hand.

Jack sharpened the axe on John's old workbench in the shed, the stone still good after all these years. The axe would be quicker and quieter than anything. He walked towards the first tree.

Inside the house, Megan and Hannah listened to the axe as they ate their breakfast. Hannah had been out to say a silent farewell to the trees that morning, had stood next to them and laid a hand on them. They had been there for as long as she could remember, and their shapes were entwined with her memories of her father. Each blow seemed to echo through the orchard, the sound carrying. Megan watched as Hannah tried not to visibly wince.

There were five in all that needed to be removed, and they could not replant without grubbing out the roots, too, as it was not the space overground that mattered, it was the lay of the soil, the obstructions that would remain there for the new roots should the old ones not be removed. There would be fungi and disease, too, which could fester and infect the new trees. So there was only one way – Hannah knew that – but it was brutal.

Megan got up, shut the door fast, and then closed the curtains at the window. 'I'll make some tea, shall I?' she asked, reading Hannah's face. Hannah nodded.

Jack pushed the tree away from him and it fell neatly. He stood a moment, catching his breath, brushed the back of his hand across his mouth. He looked at the rings inside the heartwood. Every child knew how to count the rings, but what he liked to see was whether the heartwood was centred in the tree. A tree's heart could tell you what forces it had been subjected to. If there had been a strong wind where the tree grew, the heartwood would sometimes be off-centre, having fortified itself on one side to withstand the onslaught. The rings would not just tell you how old the tree was, but what conditions it had grown in. How it had been moulded over time. This one had been sheltered, as he would expect in an orchard, but the size of the rings told him when there had been wet summers, when drought had hit, even here, over the last half-century or so.

He fetched the spade from the shed and began digging a trench around the stump. He would have to dig down on either side and cut through each root as he came to it. Slice them, and then, hopefully, with a little leverage, he could pull the stump out. He struck the soil with the spade and realized how hard it still was despite the warmer weather. The problem with stumps was that you had to remove all of them, or they would regrow; if not dealt with properly the first time, they would continue to search, looking for a way to find a foothold once more.

After lunch, Megan tried to persuade Hannah to go through to the parlour. It was quieter there and further away from the front where Jack was working. Hannah eventually acquiesced and sat in the cold room, a headache growing. This job had to be done, but that fact did not make it easier. Images of her family came to her – her father in a light short-sleeved shirt, leaning against a tree, smoking his pipe; her sister running away from her; John climbing a tree to gather mistletoe – and suddenly she felt an intense longing for what life had been. An awful loneliness that could not be alleviated with thoughts that she was doing the right thing. Each tree was a relic, witness to a time long gone, but so was she.

Hannah remained in the parlour until the weak sun had moved around the house and all the trees had been felled. When she went outside, she could see that Jack had cleared most of the trees away, but the scars were ugly in the fading light. She looked at the holes in the earth, her chest tight, tears wetting her face. Then she noticed the whips that she had planted were budding; but even the sight of the young trees taking well did not make the emptiness of the orchard any less painful.

34

MEGAN HAD ASKED HANNAH if she would go for a walk with her today. Jack would be in the orchard again, and Megan could see Hannah's agitation. Hannah had been reluctant at first, but had agreed when Megan explained that she would like to know more about the fields and lanes around Berllan-Deg. Megan had knocked on Jack's door and told him that there was some food for him on the kitchen table and that they would be back in the afternoon. Jack had understood without Megan needing to say anything explicitly and had promised that he would make everything as neat as possible by the time they came back.

They walked along the lane, talking softly as the day opened around them. The daffodils were nodding in the hedges now, the bees busier, clambering in and out, covering themselves with the startlingly bright pollen. Megan had been watching them, the way they combed it with their legs towards the storage pouches underneath them. There were primroses, too, in the shady overhangs, with a cleanliness and freshness that Megan could not get over, along with herb-robert, speedwell, and violets peeping out shyly. She had looked at John's books and learnt the Welsh and Latin names for the first time.

'People come to these places,' said Hannah, clearing her throat, 'and all they see is emptiness. Fields, hedges, nothingness. This field,' she said, pointing to the one behind Berllan-Deg, 'is Cae Pistyll. There's a

spring there. Each field has a name, a history, stories.'
Hannah's eyes warmed as her mind seemed to go back.
'You know, my mother knew my father when they were
children. They used to walk to school together. Past
these same hedges, these streams. It's strange, isn't it?
To know someone your whole life.'

Megan smiled.

'What was she like? Your mother?' asked Megan
after a moment.

'She was of her time,' answered Hannah honestly. 'I
think she did her best with what she was given, which
wasn't much.'

Megan could sense her unease.

'It's so easy to look back and judge someone,'
Hannah uttered softly.

They continued in silence for a while.

'You know, sometimes I think about the way my
mother lived, how confined the parameters were, and
the walls of my life aren't much bigger. I think people
can think that this is a small kind of life, but it can be a
deep one. Her life, my life might be invisible, but it has
meaning.' Hannah was searching Megan's face now.
'Don't you agree?'

Megan thought for a moment of how her body
had changed; how it had softened, how her neck had
stopped aching, how soundly she slept without the jolt-
ing awake and the panic. How sleep felt refreshing now
and how she stretched on awakening, arching her back
as she had done when she was a child.

'Yes,' she said, 'I do.'

*

When they arrived home, Jack had finished. The pockmarks in the orchard had been filled in, ready for the saplings to be transplanted. Even though there were gaping holes in the orchard's pattern, it looked better. Jack had sawn off most of the main branches of the trees and had roughly cut them into lengths so they could be seasoned for a year. He had lit a fire in the orchard to burn off the scraps of wood and roots and was standing next to it when they returned. Hannah thanked him silently by placing a hand on his arm as she walked past him to the house, but Megan stayed awhile, watching as he tended the fire.

Later, he asked Megan if she would mind making some coffee, and he smiled as she brought out two mugs. The sky was pale pink and orange this evening, the remaining trees silhouetted black against it. There was a new moon, cuticle-thin. Megan's eyes were drawn once more to the flames, her face warm and her body relaxed. The mesmerizing simplicity of a fire at night. Megan watched as sparks flew up into the sky and black smudges of soot seemed to hang weightless in the air. Jack also stood staring into the fire. There was a profound stillness about him, a strange peace. Megan caught his eyes for a moment through the smoke before looking quickly away.

35

HANNAH WAS EATING HER breakfast, her eyes glued to the plan on the table. Megan and Jack watched her as she smiled, put down her toast and brushed the crumbs from her fingers.

'I think it's right,' she said, touching the plan gently as if unwilling to break contact with it. 'We'll need to plant the whips first, then the trees that have been delivered.'

'They're soaking in buckets in the shed,' Jack replied.

Hannah turned over the paper. Megan could see what looked like a series of marks, some kind of punctuation she did not understand.

'There are a few that are self-pollinating, some male, some female. I've put those nearer the hives, with the others in the middle – they do better in groups, anyway.'

Jack studied the map.

'The hedges will need re-laying, too, next winter, along the borders,' said Jack. 'If that's done, it'll give more protection to the young trees in the next few years.'

'If you wouldn't mind,' said Hannah. Jack just smiled at her.

'Right, then,' he said, getting up. 'I think we should probably get started.'

He picked up the plan, looked at it in a puzzled

way, then walked out. Megan watched him go before she found Hannah's eyes on her. She got up, too.

'I'd better go and help.'

The two of them spent the morning planting the new whips, which were small and easy to transplant. The trees were all aligned north–south to provide them with as much light as possible. Hannah came out to check on progress, cutting the bandages she had wrapped the grafts in and letting them unravel a little. She would not remove them completely, as the new calluses on the trees needed to harden slowly. Jack and Megan were planting the whips slightly off-angle, but Hannah did not mind; it was her orchard now. Jack moved them around and asked Hannah if she was happy, and she would nod when she was, relying less on the grid structure than on where they looked right, and whether they were in the sun, out of any draughts. Young trees needed all the advantages they could get.

Afterwards, Megan began sorting the new trees. They were labelled clearly, and she carried them to their positions by cross-referencing with the plan. There were more eating apples, some cider ones, and big fat cooking varieties. There was the Trwyn Mochyn, which had grown in Anglesey, then an apple from Brecon called Cadwaladr; there were a pair of yellow russet apples called Marged Nicolas and a medicinal apple from Monmouth. Hannah smiled as Megan brought over the last, a young enlli apple that did not grow anywhere else in the world.

Megan placed the trees roughly where she thought

they should be and Jack and Hannah stopped by each one, finalizing the position. Then, Jack would begin to dig. Hannah insisted that the holes were dug deep and wide, much wider than the root balls. She had always thought that trees needed that room, that soft soil around them to begin with. Then a layer of dung so old it was almost soil was added, the tree was introduced to the hole and the soil packed back around it. The older trees needed to be staked, too, so that they would be supported in high winds, and keep their heartwood at their core.

They worked like this all day, until almost every tree was planted. Then they stood, looking at the orchard, the established trees sheltering the new ones, generations of trees that would nurture each other.

Megan went back to the house. Her clothes were covered in mud, so she peeled them off before changing into some things Sadie must have left behind – trousers and a shirt. She was acclimatizing to the house now, the way the sounds from the outside were so much more muffled here. Hannah had gone to fetch some food so, for the first time, Megan was alone in the empty house. It felt dark but also enveloping, a solidity in the feet-thick walls, built for generations. She had never lived in such an old house before and the life in it had surprised her, the noises and shifts, the creaks in the night. The way your journey could be tracked all through the house.

She heard footsteps and recognized them immediately, so walked back down the stairs, dipping her head to see under the low beams.

'I brought these back to you,' Jack said. He placed the pile of books on the table.

'They're John's,' Megan replied. 'I was borrowing them.'

Jack nodded.

'I'll put them back.'

They looked at each other a moment, searching for something to say.

He raised an eyebrow. 'I'll leave you to it,' he said, then turned to go.

'Have you read any of them?' she asked.

He turned back. 'They're in Welsh,' he replied. 'My grandfather spoke it, my mother didn't. I think it had to do with getting on in the world or something.' He picked up one of the books, looked at the cover and rubbed his thumb over the golden lettering. 'I can understand when I'm listening; it's the speaking. It's a pity, though . . .'

It was then that Hannah came back, pushing the door open with her shoulder, a bag in each hand. Jack moved to help her and the moment was gone.

36

SADIE HAD DRIVEN STRAIGHT to Anne's house and
knocked. Anne's car was there, and Sadie was sure
she saw a shadow through the glass panel in the door,
but she would not answer. Sadie had driven to her own
home then, the place feeling cold and empty, and called
her, but Anne didn't pick up. She had carried her hope
to Anne's door and had found it shut. She had left it too
long, and the loss hit Sadie so hard that she had been
physically sick.

She had returned the day after to find the same
response, and the day after that. Anne's silence was
deafening.

The thing that frustrated Sadie most was that she
had taken the fleeting opportunity she had been given
and abused it, and now her own selfishness stung. She
had found something so simple and had managed to
make it complicated. She would have to live with it –
the loss, the very stupidity of that loss – and now the
frustration inside her grew so that all she could do was
pace back and forth.

When she had left Seth, this house had been a haven,
a stepping stone to her future. A sterile brown house
that looked like any other, but it had been enough. Yet
now it felt lacking in every way. It was as if she had
woken up with a jolt to everything – to colour, to taste,
to pain – and she could not bear it. It was an echo of
the pain that she had felt when her childhood friend

had moved away. Back then, she had stayed in bed for days, her mother chastising her for being so dramatic; the shame she had felt, the intensity of her feelings consuming her. She had gone to that town hall dance with Hannah and John and had lost her virginity behind the hall to some boy she could not remember. Images swam before her eyes – the cider she had drunk and the rip in her tights and the headache and the body-ache and the heartache the next day. She remembered the roughness of his hands and the rumours that went around the town afterwards, which Hannah then heard. After that there had been a cycle of boy after boy, as if Sadie thought she could rub her friend's touch away from her, and then she had met Seth, and he had been everything she could ever have wanted in a husband. Shy, soft, generous, funny. They had become friends, and she had been good for him, too, made him more sociable, and it had been as good as she could have expected, but she could not have continued living like that.

She got up and poured herself a drink. She had felt other pains, too, more recently, as she looked at younger people. The ease with which they seemed to accept who they were, the families they had. A dull ache growing of a life not lived; she had to acknowledge it but that did nothing to quell her bitterness. She was old enough, too, to know that some pain was fleeting – the obsessions of youth, the end of certain friendships, even marriages – but she knew this pain; this one was soul-changing. Her confused mind flitted between the dark limbs of the orchard and the way her body had responded to Anne. She had realized it was not too late to fulfil her potential and she had been left aghast by that knowledge.

She got up. She felt the need to walk. To go. To do something. Out in the rain, the city was darkening. She fell in behind a group walking home from work, their chatter grating on her. There was a dullness to the sky here, the shock of disorientation after weeks of being in Berllan-Deg. She found the noise distracting and every street corner looked the same, making navigation confusing; the devastating sameness. She could feel her legs moving but she did not know where she was headed. It was as if she was outside her body, moving through the rain, the smeared lights, the sound. She turned down towards the canal where the rain was making circles on the water. She felt as if she was drowning now, the touch of Anne stinging her skin, on the precipice of being found and then lost again.

37

HANNAH HAD BEEN WALKING in the orchard, stopping every now and again to run her hands over the boughs and branches, feeling for buds, looking to see how each tree was doing. Despite the slowness of spring, the trees were making their preparations, little nubs and buds along each bough bursting into life. Hannah also took a sprig in her hands and bent it slightly, looking for the inflexibility and brittleness that signalled the tree had failed to take, but there were no signs of that yet. The bees had been busy in the hedgerows and the last of them were clinging to flowers in the orchard, the blooms bending under their weight. They'd have to wait a little longer for the apple blossom, but Hannah could feel that it was on the way.

The arrival of spring always used to exhaust her, its relentlessness; not that she disliked it as such. It was just that at the end of April a shift would happen, and the orchard would grow exponentially. Everything seemed fuller, greener, and the change was startling.

Inside the shed it was almost dark, and Hannah lit the single bulb that hung from the ceiling. She had been meaning to do it for a while – to add more names to the orchard on the ceiling, to update it with her own trees, along with the dates on which they were planted, the genus. She took an old crate from under the workbench and armed herself with a flat carpenter's pencil, then stepped up and began to cross away the trees they had grubbed out and add the ones they had replaced them with. Hannah's arm ached, but she was lost in the work. She had memorizèd the plan of the trees and did not need a reference. It was getting darker now and the light of the bulb seemed to glow in a circle on the ceiling. She filled the beams with dates, marks, names, but the shape of the pattern had changed. There were new clusters of trees, new constellations above her head.

The next morning, the swallows were back, chattering and wheeling above Berllan-Deg. Hannah watched them as she gathered armfuls of daffodils from the orchard, their sap wetting her fingers. When she was happy she had enough, she took the kitchen scissors from her back pocket and snipped some greenery from the elders and the hazels in the hedgerows. She had bought some white chrysanthemums from the shop, which were resting in their bright crinkly wrapping in a bucket by the door where it was coolest.

It was Flowering Sunday in a few days, and as Easter would bring full congregations in their Sunday best, Hannah knew that she could not leave the graves of her parents and John unadorned. She turned towards the house and placed the flowers in the bucket outside, then went to change her shoes. She would not change her clothes – after all, they were going to see family, and this was work. As Megan came down the stairs, Hannah was back at the sink, gathering some cloths, soap and an empty honey jar.

It was sunny today, although the wind was cold, and the breeze carried the bleating of lambs across the orchard as the two women stepped on to the road, the bucket nudging against Megan's leg with every step she took. They walked in silence, Megan's mind on John's grave and Hannah's somewhere else. Megan had passed the chapel several times on her bike and knew that her father was buried there, but she had not been in. She had stopped once, one foot on the ground, looking at its austere shape, the regimented unadorned cemetery, but she did not think it was her place to find him. It was strange, but it felt like an intrusion somehow.

'There's a tap in the corner of the cemetery. You'll need to fill up the bucket first; the graves will all need to be washed.'

Megan nodded.

'Then we'll arrange the flowers.'

The chapel was painted a light blue, with three arched windows above the door. It looked at once peaceful and restrained. Hannah pushed open the heavy black gates, their unoiled hinges protesting. She let Megan pass her and took the chrysanthemums out of the bucket before pointing to the far end of the cemetery. Megan nodded and went to fill the bucket at the tap.

Hannah walked towards the family graves – not that there were designated areas or railings as there were in some churchyards; it was just known that some families were buried in certain parts of the cemetery. As she neared her parents' grave, she reached out her fingertips instinctively, as if bringing them to mind. Then she knelt and began to weed out a few plants that had pushed their way through the gravel.

Megan made her way back towards Hannah, weaving a path through the gravestones, reading the names as she walked. She stayed back awhile, letting Hannah have some privacy, before Hannah turned and gestured for her to bring the bucket. She watched as Hannah put the cloth into the water and wrung it out, then began to clean the faces of the gravestones, making the golden lettering shine again. Hannah's mother used to do this, and her grandmother before her, each one washing the graves just as they had washed the faces of sick children or the dying. Megan knelt on the other side of the graves and began to take away the remnants of the Christmas wreath that Hannah had put there. She had seen the other mound of earth near by, without a stone, and guessed that this was John's grave, although she asked no questions and waited for Hannah's cue.

It was surprising how black the water turned – a year's worth of wind and rain and grime. Hannah dried the stones now, so that they shone under the weak sun. Then she started to arrange the chrysanthemums in the holes of a heavy marble planter. She positioned five, finding that odd numbers were always more pleasing than even ones, then filled in the gaps with daffodils before asking Megan to get more fresh water.

When someone died, the house would be filled with the scent of white lilies, a one-note perfume that was pure and clean and exquisite. Lilies would be placed first on the graves, but on Flowering Sunday you could use any flower you liked – the singularity of grief blooming into the more complex scent of loss. Daffodils, chrysanthemums, roses and freesias, each scent invoking the subtleties of longing. The bitterness of the trillium, the sweetness of the forsythia, each year bringing new memories to the fore.

Hannah pushed some greenery in with the flowers and was satisfied. Megan came back and poured some water into the marble holder. Then, Hannah turned her attention to John's grave. Megan followed her, watched as she pushed a clean honey jar down into the mound of earth, as there was nothing yet to hold the flowers and no stone to clean. Hannah cut the chrysanthemums shorter so that they would fit in the jar, then picked up the last of the daffodils and cut them to size. She added a few before stopping and handing the rest to Megan. Megan paused, tears springing to her eyes, then nodded and placed the flowers gently in the jar.

38

Swarm

There are few things we understand less than the swarm, and the beekeeper must watch for it as spring strengthens. The scientific papers say that it is the bees' way of reproducing, of splitting away from a hive that has become too large or too successful, and I believe that this might be true to some extent. There always must be a group in any society that splits away when a prevailing idea becomes too strong, a radical minority that seems to throw caution to the wind without a care for the consequences, revelling in the moment. Yet I am not sure that this seemingly sudden change of heart, this uncharacteristic recklessness, is as easily explained when it comes to bees.

After losing swarm after swarm, I began to pay more attention and realized that the bees stop bringing in nectar, and that this happens for about a week before they leave. They make preparations, some of which I don't think we will ever understand, and one morning you will come to the hive, and they will begin to pour out of it like water. Then, they will congregate and decide where to go. They keep their queen at their centre and begin scouting for a new home, resting temporarily on boughs and houses, walls and sheds. Scouts fly away from the central knot of bees and try to find new nests before reporting back, each bee trying to convince the rest that she has found the perfect new home.

If a hive is too full, you can understand their needing a new home, but I have seen it happen to young hives for no apparent reason when there is only one queen, and I think that is the key to it. We can rationalize it all we like, but I think they know that change itself is valuable. That sometimes change for change's sake is important. That breaking the usual patterns is essential for growth, that it allows them to thrive, and there is joy in that. I have seen them, Hannah – these creatures who seem so rigidly organized burn with life, with a casual anarchy. I have seen the older bees become infected by the young bees' mood and join in, and I have seen the great strength in allowing the future to work itself out. To abandon oneself, to trust the world.

It is not an easy thing to relinquish that control, but it is what I am doing now. I have two more letters, Hannah, if I can write them, and then I must relinquish everything, throw my hands in the air and become powerless. I don't think that it is a coincidence that we gain power only to lose it; it feels like we must be humbled, like we must stand on the edge of the fall as weak as we were when we came into the world.

When bees begin to swarm, they fill up their stomachs with honey to take with them in anticipation of making a new home, and therefore you will see beekeepers handle them with no gloves. They feel no threat, and want to be no threat; they are collectively and singularly in a state of joy. At their most vulnerable, they are at their gentlest.

The tawny owls are calling tonight, Hannah, but I do not fear them, not in the way I once did; rather, I feel drawn to listen to them. Their ancient cries have begun to comfort me, their huge eyes able to see what I cannot in the darkness. They do not fear it, Hannah, they do not fear it.

39

THERE WAS A LIGHT knock on the door and Megan looked up. It was Jack.

'It's still,' he said, smiling, 'and the bees are busy. I was wondering if you'd like to have a look?'

Megan smiled broadly and looked at Hannah.

'There's one of John's old suits hanging by the door,' Hannah said quietly.

Megan nodded, got up, found John's suit and followed Jack out through the door. While he lit the smoker, she pushed her legs into the suit, pulling it up over her shoulders and the veil over her head.

Jack made sure there was a steady stream of billowing smoke.

'You ready?' He grinned.

The bees were active and, as it was nearing lunchtime, a large proportion of them were already out in the orchard working. Megan had heard them as she walked towards the hive, a kind of deep alto hum that could not quite be pinpointed. She stayed back as Jack opened the crown board, and gasped as he lifted it away. The hive was teeming, the number of bees astounding; a distinct smell of amber or spice, a certain sweetness. She could also feel a deep-seated fear, something she had not known was in her, an instinctive apprehension at seeing their numbers, listening to their sounds, and she felt her heart beating in her chest. Jack watched her.

'It's uncomfortable, isn't it?' he said, reading her face.

'It's just . . .'

'Primal,' he finished her sentence.

'Yes,' she said.

'They're busy; they shouldn't cause us too many problems,' he said as he smoked the top of the frames, driving the bees down deeper into the nest. 'We want to be sure that the queen is healthy, and that there's plenty of grubs.'

Megan nodded, mesmerized by the colours on the frames as Jack held them up to the light. The bees were all around her now, butting heads with her veil. Jack saw the look on her face.

'Can they sting through the suit?' she asked.

He shrugged. 'Sometimes.'

He enjoyed her discomfort a moment, then added, 'Not often, though.'

Megan's shoulders relaxed a little and then Jack showed her a frame, pointed out what he was looking for and how he was reading it. The bees were bringing in a lot of pollen, so their brood was strong. The queen was laying thickly and everything seemed to be in order.

'We need to see the queen,' he said, straining his eyes. 'It's time for us to separate her from the honey stores. Otherwise she'll lay everywhere, if we let her, and no one needs honey with eggs in it.'

Megan crinkled her nose.

'Exactly. As the weather warms up, she'll want to dive down deep into the hive, so we'll keep the honey at the top.'

Jack pulled frame after frame from the hive, studying each one in turn, and then his face lit up. He angled the frame towards Megan.

'Can you see her?'

Megan could see nothing but a mass of bees.

'I'm not sure I can.'

'She's long, bigger than everyone else, and she has courtiers who always face her; they never turn away. Look for bees in a circle.'

Megan studied the bewildering bubbling mass of bees, but then she saw her, beautiful and shy, the other bees clustered around her as if they were bowing to her. Jack took in Megan's amazement, smiled.

After they had looked through all the hives, they closed them and let them settle down once more. Jack rolled down his suit and tied the sleeves around his waist, and Megan did the same while Jack made some coffee in the caravan. They sat for a while outside, Jack on the steps of the van, Megan on an upturned log.

'So,' he asked, 'what did you think?'

'It's like another world,' she said.

'Well, your father loved it.'

Megan looked down at her cup.

'So, how about we make a deal?' she asked, her eyes narrowing. 'You teach me about the bees, I'll teach you some more Welsh.'

Jack thought of his schooldays a moment, his father's frustration and his own embarrassment. He was not certain he could show Megan that side of him. 'I'm not sure . . .'

'Then it's no deal,' she said.

She looked away and began sipping her coffee, then sighed.

'It's a shame. I really wanted to learn more about the bees.'

Jack smiled despite himself.

Megan felt a sudden jolt of pain. She flung out her arm, and a bee flew away.

'Did she get you?' asked Jack.

Megan winced.

'Don't touch it,' he said, trying not to laugh at her almost childlike reaction.

He reached into his pocket for his penknife, flicked out the blade. He came towards her and grasped her arm. The barb was still in her skin. Megan went still.

'If you press on it, more poison will go in, make things worse.'

Megan frowned, nodded, her face serious.

Jack took the blade of the knife and scraped it along her skin. Megan could feel the steel's keenness on her forearm.

'It really hurts,' she said, looking up at him.

'It's a shock, isn't it?' He bent his head low, to check that the barb had come away, his face next to hers as he held her arm up to the light.

They stood for a moment, before she looked away and pulled back her arm.

'It'll settle in a little while,' he reassured her.

'So what do you say?' asked Megan.

'You still want to learn about them after that?'

'I'll just have to be more careful next time,' she said.

Jack looked at her and, despite his instinct to say no, he found himself softening.

'All right,' he said quietly. 'We can try.'

Hannah had been glad to have the house to herself, had sat by the fire and hardly moved all day. She had felt tired recently and, with that, her thoughts began to circle around Sadie. The fact that she hadn't heard anything; the fact that her sister hadn't returned.

There was something else growing inside her, too, a frustration that instead of saying she had missed her and had been lonely all those years as well, it had been ingrained in her to berate Sadie for not coming home before. The way she had been able to tell that there was more going on for Sadie, so much more to say. She stretched out her hand, turned the worn wedding ring on her finger around and around, her fingers having shrunk slightly with age. There were patterns that had impacted the way she had been taught to behave and it had taken Hannah so many years to see them. She felt the heaviness of the past for a moment before hearing laughter from the orchard. Jack and Megan, their voices light, intermingling. She got up and walked into John's office, laid her hand on the back of his chair.

Through the window she could see John in Megan; every day a joy and a piercing pain, the two existing together. Over the weeks, she had found the girl to be sensitive, affectionate, funny, reminding Hannah of all the things her father had been. She was his daughter in every way.

40

I N May, the dawn chorus would reach its full-throated crescendo, each bird contributing so that the orchard reverberated with sound. It was the month of growth, of effervescence. The cow parsley frothed along the hedgerows; the blossom had arrived; the sward was growing rapidly and there was such a sense of relentless burgeoning that sometimes Hannah would find herself overwhelmed by it. The lushness of the grasses, the velvetiness of the pollens and the opening of flowers so numerous that, at dawn, you could almost hear them bloom.

Hannah walked through the orchard, looking up at the blossom, its sudden arrival crowning the trees with white and pink, its freshness always startling, no matter how many times she had seen it. She had always been fascinated by the way such old trees with ancient limbs seemed to choose such saccharine delicate flowers. How, from those gnarly limbs, they could bring forth blossom that was so fragrant and so youthful. Her father used to say that it was proof that age and youthfulness could coexist, and that linear age was meaningless. Perhaps he was right, Hannah thought, considering Jack's maturity even when he was younger, and John's occasional recklessness.

Today the air was not as warm as Hannah would have liked it. Her father had shown her the stages of growth when she was a child, from the protected bud through to the mouse's ear and the late pink, when the leaves shed their fuzzy coats and the cluster of blooms branched out. After that, a lone bloom would open – a herald, if you like – signalling to the others in the cluster whether it was safe to join it.

As a child, the blossom's arrival had always brought Hannah much joy and excitement. She remembered throwing it like confetti above her head as she pretended she was getting married. Laughing as she swung on a rope under the flower-laden canopy, her head thrown back with glee. The blossom would fill the orchard with its intoxicating fragrance, and she remembered rubbing her skin with the blooms, only to be disappointed when the petals left nothing but a grassy scent. The canopy would be thick with working bees, so much so that the whole orchard would take up a distinct strum. And then, when the blossom fell, it would blow across the orchard in snowstorms, catching in drifts and filling the air with colour, and Hannah would run through it, kicking up the flowers with pure joy. Her bed, the bath, her shoes would be full of petals until, as suddenly as it had arrived, the blossom would disappear.

The new trees which Hannah had grafted had all taken, their single whips covered in tender leaves, and the new trees she had bought were also doing well. One or two had blossom on them, although when they fruited, she would pinch off the apples so that they could concentrate on growth. She would not take any fruit from them until they were mature and established. She walked among them, feeling pleased that they had got this far. They would need fair weather now, no sudden frosts that could devastate whole crops.

She walked towards the shed and pushed open the door. She had been keeping used tea leaves in a bucket of water here, and she also added some blood and bone-meal which they kept for ailing trees. Her father had tried all sorts of tonics over the years, some passed down from older generations, others he had made up himself. Hannah took the old watering can and tipped the contents of the bucket into it. She straightened her back and carried it out to the orchard, and walked around each of the young trees, feeding them as she went.

Megan had been spending more time in Jack's caravan. She would carry books there after supper every evening and Hannah would hear her come back late at night. This morning someone had called at the caravan saying that there was a swarm in the village, and Jack had come to fetch Megan. A swarm in May was worth collecting, as they could rehouse it and the colony would have enough time to establish itself and make honey before the winter. Hannah smiled, thinking of the two of them doing the same thing she and John had done so many times.

Hannah lingered outside until Jack's van returned. She watched as he carried the swarm gently towards the hives. Megan came to stand beside her.

'It's strange, isn't it?' said Hannah. 'How they leave the safety of home like that, throw themselves on the mercy of the world.'

'I think they've found a good home,' replied Megan, holding Hannah's gaze.

'John always thought swarms were a sign of good luck.'

'Let's hope they'll be happy,' Megan replied, crossing her arms in front of her. There was a cold breeze and a wind coming from the east, which always unsettled Hannah.

'Let's hope so,' she replied.

The sky had been grey in the city for days and for the first time Sadie noticed that there were no real seasons here, or at least she did not feel them in the same way. There were falling leaves, of course, parks to sit in in summer, but nature was dampened down, pushed to the edge of a world which stayed fundamentally, artificially, the same. Her time at Berllan-Deg had sharpened her senses, made her more attuned to the subtleties of the changing light – how it was muddied by street lamps, how the air here caught in her throat and the way she felt suffocated by it.

For days now she had been reaching out to Anne only to be met with silence, and after watching the day fade once again she realized that there was something other than the loss of Anne making her feel uneasy. She turned, switched on a lamp and, with the growing light, she realized what it was. She wanted to go home. She packed quickly, pulled the door closed behind her and started the car. For the first time in her life, the word held some meaning for her. Perhaps it was strange, but she had not noticed that she had rooted a little until she left the orchard, and now, without Anne, she needed Berllan-Deg more than ever. She had dreamt about it, too, the trees now lighter, airier somehow. In so many ways, she had not lived there before. Not really. Versions of Sadie had: a lonely child, a young girl full of shame, an estranged sister and a disconnected wife who came to visit with Seth. This feeling she had was new, like she was beginning to understand the idea of home in her body. She drove down the familiar lanes through the darkest part of the night, and, as the headlights swung into the orchard, she remembered all those times she used to wait for Hannah to come home. She resolved to wake her in the morning, speak with her.

She got out of the car, a half-moon lacing the edge of the trees around her. It was still, the orchard seemingly holding its breath. She moved towards the trees and, as she walked, she realized how cold it was. She looked up. All the stars were visible; it was completely cloudless. Then, suddenly, she felt her bag fall from her hand. She looked down at it and began to feel a dizziness; there was something wrong with her vision, too, and she felt a sudden wash of dullness run through her. She couldn't think. It was then, on the cusp of dawn, that she fell.

41

A COLD DAWN HAD broken, grey and misty, and the blossom was dangerously shrunken; there was a crispness in the air and on the grass. Jack had risen early, concerned about the orchard and the bees. He had put some blankets around the hives and had walked the orchard feeling the flowers, wondering whether they were too cold. Then, he had glanced towards Berllan-Deg, its whitewashed face looking bluish in the early light, and seen Sadie on the orchard floor. Heart leaping, he had carried her into the house, shouting for Megan and Hannah, then placed her by the fire as he desperately sought some blankets. Megan had appeared wide-eyed, her hands shaking, and Hannah had descended the stairs in shock behind her. Jack had asked Megan to rekindle the fire and run to John's office to ring for help.

Jack had met the ambulance out on the road and had helped them close the back doors. Almost as soon as they had arrived, they were gone again, taking Sadie with them. Jack stood in the road watching them go, Megan trying to comfort Hannah behind him. As the stillness settled around them once again, Megan led Hannah back to the house.

It was cold, too cold, and Jack did not know what else to do. He had done all he could for Sadie but now, as he looked at the orchard around him, another strange, deep-seated fear settled inside him. He had seen years like this, a sharp frost coming out of nowhere, and the harvest would be non-existent. In years gone by, it had not made too much of a difference, but Jack had heard the way Hannah talked about the orchard now, listened to how she spoke about it, the way her fingers would trace the plans on the table. He knew how vulnerable the young trees were. He paced, and then he walked abruptly to the remaining pile of brash and dead wood which Hannah had cut from the trees. He dragged some wood to the middle of the orchard, then returned to fetch some more. He heard the door to Berllan-Deg open and a figure came towards him. It was Megan, dressed now, her face pale, her arms crossed in front of her.

'They say they'll call us; it looks like it was some kind of stroke.'

Jack nodded. 'I can take Hannah to see her when they know which ward she'll be on. Until then, there's nothing to do but wait.'

Megan was studying him. 'What are you doing?'

'It's too cold; we'll lose the blossom.'

Megan looked aghast, her skin already dampening in the cold.

'We need to light fires,' he continued. 'All around, to warm the air.'

'And what about the bees?' asked Megan.

'I've closed the entrances,' he said. 'Come on.'

Megan nodded, saw what needed to be done, and helped him build piles of old wood here and there throughout the orchard. Then, when they were ready, Jack fetched some petrol he had in a jerrycan, and they lit the fires one at a time until the whole orchard was aflame. When they had finished, they stood, the warmth rolling off the fires around them, making the air shimmer with heat.

Hannah sat looking out at the orchard. The smoke had permeated the kitchen, as the windows were old and draughty. Hannah guessed what Jack was doing and was silently thankful for it, for his trying to keep the blossom alive.

She felt a familiar fear again this morning, a fear she had not expected to be experiencing again so soon. Losing John had made her realize how little she had known him, and she could not bear to feel the same with her sister, to lose her without knowing her. She could still see her now, pale, cold, her brown hair unbrushed, her little sister with the same upturned mouth she had as a child.

Hannah got up slowly and made her way to the window, watched as the orchard came in and out of focus, the smoke rolling across it, the fires casting an eerie glow. She had watched her mother wait as her father died; she herself had waited by John's side, the humbling hours in which no one could do anything. She had known with certainty what the outcome of those waits would be, but today the uncertainty was unbearable. She felt a sorrow and an anger, too, saw images of a laughing Sadie as a child, running through the orchard; Sadie asleep on their father's lap as he read; her defiance, her natural exuberance. She looked out and watched as the soft blossom was slowly engulfed in smoke.

42

HANNAH WAS OUT IN the orchard for the first time in days. It was warm, with a light breeze. The fires that Jack and Megan had lit had left black circles all through the grass, and the wind was agitating the ashes. Hannah felt the light on her skin like water, a long drink she had thirsted for after watching Sadie for so long.

Sadie had eventually pressed Hannah's fingers, a slow returning to consciousness. Her eyes had fluttered open, and Hannah had kissed her forehead. She was still weak, her voice a mere whisper, but she was gaining strength. She had been brought home the day before and, although pale, her arm a little unnaturally stiff, she was still Sadie.

Now Hannah examined the blossom. Some blooms were edged with brown, but the majority had been saved. Cluster upon cluster still to open. Hannah felt a relief wash through her and found there were tears on her cheeks, the tension that she had held so long releasing with the waking of Sadie and the sight of the blossom. She noticed that the new trees were thriving, too, and the old ones had redoubled their efforts to grow, had pushed out new shoots, tender stems, and were reconfiguring their shape.

Over the past few days, Megan had been fetching errands from the village, hanging shopping bags from the handles of her bike, and cooking. In doing so, she had relieved the pressure on Hannah so that she could sit with Sadie, and she had also been helping Jack with the hives. He wanted to take a hive to the uplands this year, as John used to do, and had been asking around for those people with higher ground, the rent of the plot usually paid with an agreed amount of honey.

When Hannah turned back towards the house, she saw Sadie in the doorway, a blanket around her shoulders. She had lost weight, was leaning on her stick, but she looked well. Sadie walked out into the orchard.

'You're not supposed to be . . .'

'Pshh,' Sadie answered, smiling tiredly. She was still pale, ashen. 'Fresh air, isn't that what they say?'

They stood a moment in silence.

'Will you sit with me, Hannah?' she asked, studying Hannah seriously. Sadie's voice was weaker, breathier. It would take time for it to strengthen.

Hannah nodded, and they sat on two chairs that Megan and Jack had placed in the orchard.

'I want to tell you why . . .' Sadie said slowly. 'I want to tell you what I . . . I've not been honest with myself, or you.'

Hannah frowned, but didn't look at her, scared of what was to come.

Sadie wondered how she could articulate a lifetime's longing, the feeling that her heartwood was off-centre.

'I was ill because I wasn't happy, and I wasn't happy with Seth . . . because I wasn't myself . . .'

Hannah could sense Sadie feeling for the words.

'I met someone else and fell in love . . .'

Hannah turned her head now.

'And she was a woman.'

Hannah listened and felt the words falling into place.

'I fell in love with a woman, and I wouldn't accept it . . . and now she . . .'

Sadie dropped her head to her chest and Hannah realized she was overcome.

'She doesn't want to see me any more.'

Sadie's heartbreak was palpable.

'I didn't want you to think that I was someone else, or that you didn't know me, and after John, the way it changed how you saw him, I didn't know what to do.'

Sadie lifted her head and saw silent tears on Hannah's face.

'Hannah?'

Nothing.

'Hannah, say something.'

Hannah looked back at the orchard.

'You know, every single apple contains the material to make a completely new kind of apple.'

Sadie stared at her, confused.

'Father taught me that if we didn't graft trees, every apple in the world would be its own distinct variety. It seems that it is only men who value sameness.' Hannah smiled. 'They worry about lineage, genus, straight lines. I don't think women do, not in the same way.'

Hannah thought a moment.

'The Eden they gave us was so narrow.'

Sadie couldn't speak, but she reached out and Hannah did the same, and they sat clasping hands.

43

SPRING HAD MATURED IN the orchard and now the hedgerows were swelling into summer. The fruit had set in hard knots on the trees and was beginning to grow. Hannah had walked to the village early, made small talk with some neighbours, then had come back and placed some breakfast and a newspaper on a tray. She walked up the stairs, trying to hold the tray steady. The bedroom door was slightly ajar, so she pushed it with her elbow.

Sadie had been asleep for days, the weight of all she had been carrying, and her own learnt resistance, finally put down. Hannah had never known her sister to rest like this. She walked in, and saw her stirring.

'Good morning,' she said. Sadie rubbed her eyes like a child, her face breaking into a half-smile on seeing Hannah. She pulled herself up to sitting. Hannah waited patiently and passed her the tray, then sat down beside her. They looked out at the burgeoning orchard, the new trees beginning to make their presence felt, and the sound of the birds mixing with Megan's and Jack's voices.

'What are they doing?' asked Sadie.

'They've had this idea to plant some shrubs, flowers for the June gap, to help the bees. They're planting yarrow and larkspur and goodness knows what.'

Sadie looked puzzled.

'In the old flowerbeds?'

Hannah nodded. The beds had been their mother's, and Hannah had not planted anything in them all these years. They had covered themselves with a sward and almost disappeared.

'Do you remember those dahlias?' asked Sadie, smiling.

Hannah didn't answer, but they sat in a contented silence.

'I could never think less or differently of you,' Hannah said eventually. 'I wish I had made it safe enough for you to tell me. And you love this woman?' she asked.

Sadie's eyes closed imperceptibly from the pain of thinking about her.

'Yes . . .'

Hannah considered this, her fingers entwined around her cup.

'And since we're being honest, Hannah, John knew . . . that I liked women.'

Hannah turned towards her sharply.

'He didn't . . . He didn't do anything wrong. But I begged him not to tell anyone.'

There was a new sorrow in Hannah's eyes now, and Sadie regretted having told her.

'He guessed. When I was . . . what? Sixteen. I don't think he thought it was serious, and then I got married and that was that.'

Hannah looked less tense now.

'There wasn't space for it, the language for it, around here – you know that.'

Hannah nodded imperceptibly.

'He didn't do anything wrong. He tried to help.'

Hannah looked down at her tea. 'We're so vast, each of us. You remember when you said that?'

There was laughter in the orchard now and Sadie smiled listening to it.

'I remember you and John like that, chasing each other around those trees. That excitement, that life.'

'So what will you do about this woman?'

'Anne?' asked Sadie. 'There's nothing I can do but accept it.'

'Don't carry it any more, Sadie, please. You told me to put my grief somewhere or it would kill me. You'd do well to do the same.'

44

IN JUNE, THE TREES would let go of some of their fruit, would shed what they did not need and put their energy into what they did. Even so, more fruit would need to be picked so that what was left could grow to its full potential, the trees somehow always overestimating the burden that they could bear. Jack hauled out the two ladders that John had stored in the rafters of the shed and carried them outside.

It had been quiet at Berllan-Deg in the last few days. Megan had been busy looking after Hannah and Sadie, and Jack had felt her absence, had found his eyes drawn towards the house every now and again. He had become used to their reading time together, the way Megan would carry over mugs of coffee, books clutched haphazardly under her elbow. The way that she had practised Welsh words with him, enunciating them. He had always felt an intense embarrassment at school, a strange shame that seemed to come from not being able to decipher the words, how he would have difficulty with the soundscape he'd heard but not felt in his mouth. With her, the language was alive, shifting the air around them, and he was learning quickly, pieces of himself falling into place. Megan would repeat the words, and, listening to her, he had not just approximated them, he had owned them. He found himself thinking through her voice, thinking about her mouth, and when she left in the evening, there was a certain emptiness in the caravan that he had not noticed before.

He picked up a ladder to carry towards the nearest tree, resting it on a sturdy branch, then climbed up to start work. The trees had fruited well and were reluctant to let any of their apples go, but Jack pinched the excess away, then moved the ladder round and started on the other side of the tree.

He heard the door of Berllan-Deg open and looked down through the leaves to see Megan walking towards him, in a pair of overalls she had borrowed from Sadie. Jack smiled on seeing her, the rolled-up sleeves and the mess of hair.

'What?' Megan asked.

'Nothing,' he replied.

'So,' she said grinning, 'what do you want me to do?'

She had her hands on her hips, her face gaining more colour as the year wore on.

'What we'll be doing is pinching off these smaller apples here . . . see? Can you see the difference between this and this?'

Megan nodded, then frowned. 'Not really.' She laughed and Jack rolled his eyes, stepped down the ladder.

'You go up,' he said. 'You'll see better.'

She climbed up slowly and he climbed after her, reaching past her, his chest to her back.

'So, there's five fruits here,' he said. 'What you're looking for is potential. Leave this one here and pinch off the rest.'

Megan realized how close he was, his breath next to her ear, lost in his concentration on the apples until he, too, pulled back a little. He felt her nearness a moment more, before descending the ladder and clearing his throat.

'I'll start on another tree,' he said, turning away.

Megan felt the heat flush on her neck as, through the canopy, she watched him walk away.

Sadie had begun to write. She had thought about what Hannah had said, thought about her own inability to speak, and had decided to put it into words. She had been filling pages for days and days, in no particular order; there was no start or middle or end, but the process had made her feel lighter. She had written about her friend when she was a child, about Seth and her own feelings, and then, when she had finished, she had begun writing letters, to her father and her mother, defining and redefining their relationship. The night before, when Hannah had gone to bed, she had sat next to the fire and fed the letters to it, letting each one catch, watching as the flames walked their way across the surface of the paper before consuming it.

Today, she wanted to write the last letter. To Anne. She had been thinking about what she would say, how she could put into words how she had come to meet herself when she was already closer to the end of her life than the beginning. The insight and the pain that this had caused. She tried to catch what she felt, knowing that it wasn't enough, and then she sealed it in an envelope, addressing it to Anne. Then, she got up, walked through the orchard towards the hedgerow where the old tin was. She had to respect Anne's wishes, but she needed somewhere to lay her troubles.

45

J ACK HAD WOKEN EARLY to close the door of the hive
and stop the bees flying. It was warm, and he knew
that, given a chance, they would be out working early.
He had taped the entrance shut and tied straps around
the body of the hive. He waited for Megan to come from
the house so they could carry the hive together to the
back of the van. The first of July was the first day they
could put a hive on the uplands, and he had found the
perfect place. Megan had made a picnic and put it in
the van for when their work was done.

Megan sat in the passenger seat, her hair tied up, as
Jack drove, a strange tension in the van that only carrying a hive of live bees could induce. The landscape
outside the window changed as they moved out of the
valley, the softness of the land sharpening, the number
of trees lessening, the gradient rising. Megan had never
been in the uplands before. She took everything in,
greedy for exploring a new place. Jack watched her out
of the corner of his eye, amused by her enthusiasm. The
green grassland now gave way to coarser grass, yellowed
over the years by the harshness of the wind, and winding roads seemed to appear out of nowhere as the way
ahead was obscured by turn after turn. And then, the
open vistas, huge and humbling, the occasional sheep
or stone wall giving a sense of scale. Jack drove up a
narrow track and Megan could not conceal her delight.

There was a sea – a sea of purple heather, for what

seemed like miles. Jack turned off the engine and smiled at her. She stepped out of the van. It was breath-taking, the colour intense, shot through with violet and pink, the valley floor far below them. Megan stooped down to take a closer look and saw that every plant was a collection of a thousand bell-shaped flowers.

'Come on, then,' Jack said, pulling on his bee suit. Megan did the same, balancing on one foot as she pushed the other into the trouser leg, then zipping it up under her chin, pulling the veil over her head.

'Let's be careful,' said Jack. 'It's hard to know where you're putting your feet up here.'

Megan smiled and they took hold of a side of the hive each, then gingerly carried it through the heather. Jack had laid a platform of wood to keep it level when he had chosen the site, and they now placed the hive on top of it, their eyes meeting as it touched the planks.

'We'll let them out?' asked Megan. Jack pushed his veil back from his face.

'Not yet,' he said, pinching the fingers of one glove to take it off. 'Imagine if you'd had your routine disrupted, been kidnapped and left somewhere completely new.'

'I kind of have,' she said, smiling.

'Fair point, but let's give them a chance to settle for a while.'

The day was warm and the woody fragrance of the heather began to rise up around them, the stonechats chattering. Megan took off her suit, too, while Jack pointed out all the cottages and the farms in the distance, most of them difficult to see as they hunkered down into the landscape. He could name every rise and fall; each face of the mountain had a name and a story and a path and a trail. He told her of the dangers, too, the people who had died here, in snow and ice, in shafts that fell hundreds of feet below them. The deceptiveness of the landscape in this clement weather.

Without thinking, Jack took her hand and started to lead her towards a spring he knew.

'They'll need water, and this is the best,' he said as they came to an unremarkable dark mark on the mountainside. A small deep pool. He let go of Megan's hand and knelt, took a palmful of water. Megan did the same. It was piercingly cold.

'You'd never think that this turns into a stream further down, and that then turns into a river, the one that runs through the village.'

Megan looked at Jack, the way he navigated this place, a certainty to him that she could not fathom. He glanced up and caught her eye, which made her look away a moment.

'Shall we let them out?' he said.

Jack listened to the bees and was happy that they were calmer, so he pulled up some grass from the ground near the hive. He balled it up and unstrapped the hive, then untaped the entrance. He opened the door, pushing the grass into the doorway as the bees began to emerge.

Megan looked at him, puzzled.

'They'll have to stop and think,' he said. 'The grass will bring them to the present, make them realize they're in a different place.'

Megan and Jack watched as the bees began to squeeze through, reorientating themselves as they went, the noise of the hive increasing as the novelty of their situation was communicated. The scouts made exploratory flights back and forth, returning excitedly every now and again with news of more and more pollen.

Megan and Jack watched until the sun climbed overhead, making the suits swelteringly hot. They moved away from the bees, peeled off the suits and went to fetch their lunch. Jack had some coats in the back of the van and he laid them down on the springy brash heather. Then they spent the afternoon sitting in the sun. They were in no rush – there was little else to do today – and Megan had taken off her shoes and rolled up her trousers. The ground beneath them was warm, the noise of life below carrying on without them intoxicating.

'I'm glad Sadie is happier now,' said Megan quietly.

Jack pulled his jumper over his head then lay down, his body aching slightly after the previous day's work. He rested a hand on his face to shield his eyes from the sun, listened to her voice.

'I don't think it's uncommon, though.'

'What?' asked Jack, his eyes closed now. Megan looked down at him. His temples, the side of his mouth.

'To . . . I don't know . . . to live one kind of life while wishing for another.'

She was tired, too, so she lay down beside him, and he felt the shock of her head on his shoulder, her burning nearness, as they both listened to the world turn around them.

46

HANNAH HAD WASHED ALL the jars in hot soapy water and laid them out on the table. She would bring out an old wallpaper-pasting table for the job and place old newspaper on the floor. Jack and Megan had been adding supers to two of the hives and they were ready to be lifted. The old metal honey-spinner was in the kitchen, and Sadie supervised as Megan washed it thoroughly, making sure that the tap at the bottom was clean.

The taking of honey was never easy – having worked so hard for it, it was natural for the bees to want to protect it. However, Jack had found that the earlier you took it, the better. It was as if the bees knew that they had enough time to make up their stocks, that summer somehow was ongoing.

He had waited until midday before taking the roofs off the hives, when most of the bees would be outside, hard at work. Megan helped him and, for once, he had to use smoke to push the bees further into the hives so that he could extract the full frames of honey without taking a number of bees as well. The full frames were heavy, each cell packed with honey and sealed with wax, the workmanship exquisite. Jack took out frame after frame and handed them to Megan, who placed them into an empty box, shooing away any stray bees with her glove. The disturbance had made a great number of them fly around, although Jack was happy that their tone was irritated rather than angry. More than anything, they seemed indignant about the interruption to their work. Jack made sure that they had enough stores for the winter, even if the rest of the summer was wet, and replaced the full frames with some empty ones. He then closed the hive before repeating the process with the next one.

After they had finished, there was a cloud of bees at the bottom of the orchard. Jack threw a cloth over the full frames, as the bees were naturally drawn to the honey's scent and would try to follow and protect it. Together, he and Megan carried the frames towards Berllan-Deg, the weight of them meaning that they had to carry a side of the box each. They closed the door of the farmhouse, but even then some stray bees had managed to follow them in, which made Hannah stand and wave her arms around while Jack gently tried to guide them towards the door.

Hannah had a pot of water boiling on the stove, and into it she put what looked like a long knife, so it would be clean and hot. Sadie smiled as Jack took off his suit then began to slice the cappings from the cells. As he did so, Megan gasped. The honey was startling, oozing out of every cell, each slice Jack took away revealing the abundance of honey below. He slotted the frame into the spinner and repeated the step over and over, returning the knife to the boiling water every now and again in order to keep it warm enough to cut through the wax cleanly. Megan, unable to stop herself, reached out her finger and smudged it into the drops of honey that, despite Hannah's preparations, covered the table.

Then, Hannah spun the honey. Megan watched as the cells flowed down the sides of the barrel, the amount staggering. Jack took the empty frames. He said that, in time, he would replace them in the hives, as there was repair work to be done on them, and the bees were the best ones to undertake it. They would clean up the frames, rebuild the cells, their appetite for restoration limitless.

After he had finished, the whole kitchen smelt different, an intense spiciness and a sweetness that Megan had never experienced before. Hannah buttered some bread and they all sat together, smearing it with honey and eating in contented silence, Hannah and Sadie watching as Megan and Jack occasionally caught each other's eye.

In the afternoon, after the honey had settled, Hannah helped Jack pour it into jars. Megan watched as it snaked its way, full of air bubbles at first, then settling into a golden stillness. They filled one jar after another, Hannah sealing them, Megan placing them in boxes. Then the clean-up began. Megan was surprised at how sticky everything was; there was honey on the floor, on the table, on their clothes, and it took scalding water to get everything clean. Hannah gathered up the newspapers and Sadie watched as Megan washed the outside of the jars with clean hot water.

Jack seemed tired and he left as Hannah and Sadie helped themselves to a supper of more bread and honey. Megan joined them. When they had finished, Sadie and Hannah went to bed, but Megan could not rest. She had been aware of where Jack was in relation to her all day; where he was looking, what he was saying, and what he was not. She had felt so at peace here, had shed her constant anxiety, but this – this tension was new. She sat by the cold fireplace, watching as the late-summer light lit up the room like amber. Everything coming into focus. The jars of honey, the table, and the orchard beyond. She could see the light in the caravan illuminating the orchard. She went out and walked towards it.

Jack was already lying down when he heard the knock at the door. He pulled himself up and went over to answer it, smoothing down his hair with one hand as he did so. Outside, he saw Megan, a question on her face. She came towards him, and he found himself with his hand on her neck, kissing her, felt her pressing against him. He leant over her head and closed the door behind her, keeping out the cold.

47

MEGAN AND JACK SPENT the next day together, not leaving the caravan. They had enough food and the world could wait. The warmth of the past few days had broken, illuminating the sky occasionally with thunderless lightning, before dissolving into a light rain which darkened the orchard. Jack had woken first, surprised to find Megan wound around his arm, her thigh on his, and he had lain there awhile, unwilling to break the spell. He listened to her exhaling, caught the smell of her hair. Then, he gently extricated himself and went to make some coffee.

He could live like this; he knew he could. He could wake like this every day and be entirely content. The naturalness of her intrusion into his life scared him – his willingness to give over his space, his routine – yet he would not think twice. He poured the coffee and went to slice some bread, opened the cupboard, took out a jar of honey.

'What kind is that?' It was her voice, sleepy.

Jack smiled, spread the honey on to the bread and brought it to her.

'Last year's.'

She bit into it and frowned. 'Tastes like dandelions.'

'You're right.' He kissed her neck, then had a sudden thought. 'Wait a minute,' he said. 'Stay there.'

He disappeared back to the cupboard and Megan heard jars clinking. She laughed as he came back with a scarf in his hand, which he tied over her eyes.

'What are you doing?'

She could feel his arms around her.

She heard him opening a jar, the scrape of a spoon on the rim.

'Try this.'

She opened her mouth. The spoon was cold and the honey was sharp, stringent like lemon. Megan wrinkled her forehead, her senses heightened by the blindfold.

'It's an early one, mainly tree pollen,' said Jack, looking at her mouth, the curve of her smile.

'I wouldn't expect that.'

'If you close your eyes, you get past your expectations, what you've been told honey should taste like. Try this one.'

Another jar opening, the spoon in her mouth. This one was thicker, drier, and she had to scrape the honey off the spoon with her teeth.

'That comes from the uplands. It's not heather honey, though.'

Megan let the honey sit on her tongue and she could taste the peat, the harsher landscape, the world outside the orchard. He kissed her again.

'That was a palate cleanser,' he whispered. 'And this one, I won't tell you.'

The scent of flowers filled Megan's mouth.

'It tastes like here.'

'You're right,' he replied, resting his forehead against hers. He pressed his thumb to her mouth.

'What do you want, Megan?' he asked suddenly. 'I've been thinking about it: you came here, you stayed here, but what do you want next?'

'I want . . .'

'Think before you answer me, please. Tell me the truth.'

Megan thought, his closeness excruciating.

'I don't know,' she answered finally. 'I've spent so long not feeling anything, only this nervousness, this feeling in my stomach that something was wrong, but now that that's gone, I want to feel safe.'

Jack considered this, fighting the heaviness in his chest. His father's admonishments over the years coming back to him. She waited a moment, not knowing what he was thinking, before pulling the scarf from her eyes, the taste of honey still blooming in her mouth.

48

Bitter Honey

As a child, I thought honey to be sweet, would ask my mother for some every morning, and she would give it to me, the taste so painfully saccharine. It was only as I grew older, as my tastes and understanding changed, that I realized that honey contains colours, Hannah; it contains landscapes and feelings. I have tasted a heather honey, pungent and treacle-like, that held summer storms within it, the smoke of peat and the uplift of the lark. I have tasted late-flowering honeys, a certain urgency of flavour in them, concentrated as if the bees knew that their time for harvesting was coming to an end. I have tasted golden honeys collected with ease, but that still had a sourness to them, or a saltiness that underscored the sweetness. I would be wary of anyone who says that honey is sweet.

I remember, when I was young, my father lining the jars up on the kitchen windowsill, the light catching them so that they cast butterscotch rays across the room, and their colours, Hannah, from gold to orange through to burnt umber and sienna with a touch of green, some opaque, some crystallized, others clear. My father said that some of the old keepers would take honey frequently, depending on which flowers the bees had been harvesting from, so that they could harness the honey as medicine, frame by frame, cell by cell.

Perhaps it is all of our journeys, or perhaps some people can taste that bitterness earlier. My love for you was simple to begin with; it lacked depth, knowledge. It was nature, and the strength of it, the overwhelming cloyingness of it, made it so that I could think of nothing else, and I opened my mouth and asked you to feed it to me like a child. The energy it gave me was intoxicating, thrilling, and I loved you for it, but it was only after we were married that I saw your strength, your reserve. The way you had changed. And I felt responsible for that, but I loved you all the more for it, too. There were top notes of apple blossom that seemed to run through your veins, but there were roots underneath. You learnt to withstand me; you would not give in to me. You challenged me, and I you, infuriating you with the things I said. You made me despair sometimes, with your reservedness, that seam of coldness you have within you. You withstood so much, you grieved for so much, you loved so much, but you did so in your own way.

Some cultures place honey in a baby's mouth, while others daub it on the lips of those who are dying, and I can understand this. I do not believe in a God, Hannah, but I think that honey can tell us everything we need to know about living and about dying. If we can understand its complexity, we can understand our surroundings, we can understand our climate and how the bees feel. If we can do all of this, then we can understand that all the best things are both bitter and sweet, that there is no light without darkness and no love without loss.

I am getting weaker, Hannah; I have one letter left for you, then I must let you go. There is an ache inside me just thinking about it. We had breakfast together this morning; I don't know if you will remember this, but Jack was there and he cut some comb for us, and we ate it together. It gives me comfort that he will be there for you, and I know that he is a better man at heart than I could ever be. He believes that I have taught him things, when in fact it is he who taught me.

It is getting colder now; even the thick walls of Berllan-Deg cannot keep out the winter for ever. I am finding it harder to write; my thoughts are not so ordered. Perhaps that is how it goes: that language, that thoughts will come and go now, in no particular order, so that time itself begins to break up, and even the present is fractured. If I wake tomorrow, Hannah, and we both know that it is not a given, I will ask you for some honey. As I have done so many times. And I will rejoice in its bitterness, and I will tell you again, Hannah, that you are loved.

49

JACK TRIED TO KEEP away from Megan, but she seemed to be everywhere, even when she was not. In the smell of his clothes, in his thoughts, in what he ate, how it tasted. The vulnerability he had heard in her voice pressing on him, the shame of his body promising something he couldn't fulfil. He could not offer her anything more than himself and he could not ask anyone to live as he did, yet he had still taken something from her. He felt he had never accomplished much, but he had always been a man defined by his actions.

He picked up his bag from the floor and began to stuff a few clothes into it, consoling himself with the thought that she had been tentative around him after staying the night, a little reserved. He had some work to finish which was some miles away, and he could not think when she was near. He yanked the drawstring of the bag tight, slung it over his shoulder, and closed the door of the caravan behind him. Summer had filled in the orchard's canopy, so that his movements would be invisible from the house, and for that he was thankful. He threw his bag into the back of the van and then drove out into the lane.

There had been a few girls, over the years, in the village. One who had moved away to college and never come back, which happened a lot in a place where the allure of leaving was so strong and the reasons to stay so few. He'd seen an older woman, too, for a while, but she had become impatient with his nomadic lifestyle, as his father had warned him that they all would, so things had come to a natural end.

He had not really observed love, only attachments. His father's frustration towards his mother, the casual relationships that seemed to fill some of his old friends' lives. The closest he had come was watching John and Hannah, their wordless touches, and then had come the news of Megan, which had troubled him. The fact that Hannah would be so hurt, although he had never been one to pry. Had he not dismissed the notion of a family already, the thought that John could have harboured such a secret would have made the idea even more impossible. Yet still, there was something else making him uneasy. Something about being near her that made him want to be careful, like handling bees on a thundery day, every cell in his body warning him of something. He would feel a trembling deep inside him, for he knew that he could not give her what she needed and what she deserved.

That evening, Hannah went to sit outside on the cornerstone where her father used to sit. She took in the familiar view he had had over those long years. It was getting dark now, the last long beams of light dappling the orchard floor. The cow parsley was luminous in the hedges, the spiderwebs silvering the long grass, the apples beginning to harden off. The first harvest was in, and Hannah felt grateful for it and revelled for a moment in the silence. Hannah could see how she had become quieter over the years, her ebullient chatter dying down as she grew unsure of the effect of her words on men.

When her mother was dying, Hannah had become almost silent, had tended and nursed wordlessly. There had been nothing more to be said, nothing she could do that would please her mother. Hannah thought that this must have been around the time when Megan was born. After the funeral, John had seemed more present than he had been for years. Suddenly, they had a home for themselves, a place to be at ease. She remembered the way he would bring her tea, whisky sometimes with warm water, the way he had coaxed her back to speaking. If she were honest, perhaps she had thought at the time that something had changed, but she had not had the strength to question what it was. They would sit together at the table, her feet on his, she would touch his shoulder as he sat reading, and it did not hurt more now that she knew Megan had been a child then.

She remembered one dry September day when they had dragged some of her parents' old things outside and burnt them in the orchard. Hannah had been exhausted, the years of caring showing in the hunch of her back, and she had looked over to see John, tears falling down his face.

After that, save for the absence of Sadie in Hannah's life, they had grown together. Hannah had softened; John had tended to her. They would sit listening as the trees creaked outside or as April winds swept through the new leaves in the orchard. He would read his work in progress to her, and she would listen. The touch of their hands, silent exclamations; a tap on the shoulder, a comma; a look, a full stop. During this time, John's work had matured, been recognized, and Hannah had begun to speak more about her wishes, her wants.

Resisting the world had become second nature to her; her difficulty had been in staying soft in a world that was so hard.

50

MEGAN HAD BEEN OVER to the caravan again this evening. It was empty; he still wasn't back. She had stood looking at the closed door, feeling the damp air cling to her skin, before winding her way back through the orchard, the boughs of the trees starting to droop under the weight of fruit. The orchard was heavy, ripening, at its most beautiful. Everything was at ease, except Megan. She found one of the chairs in the orchard and sat.

She had felt Jack's manner change after they had been together, a certain coolness creeping in. She had sensed it in the slight aversion of his eyes when he had taken off the blindfold. It was as if he had seen her vulnerability and been repelled by it. Her stomach lurched with how honest she had been, how fragile her voice had sounded. How, although she had not been with a man for so many years, it had all felt as easy as breathing. But then he had left.

She heard uneven footsteps behind her, the squeeze of a hand on her shoulder as Sadie leant on her cane to sit. Megan glanced at her sideways, said nothing. Sadie had raised her eyebrows in understanding when she had seen Megan come into the house the morning after staying with Jack. Hannah had busied herself with the dishes, had chosen to mind her own business. The next morning, Sadie had found the caravan empty. When she had come back into the house to tell Hannah, it had been obvious from the look on Megan's face that she had not expected his departure either.

'The thing about Jack is, he'll show you who he is. He'll be thinking about something. Doing something. It's just not his way to talk about things,' said Sadie.

'That's what I'm scared of,' said Megan instinctually.

Sadie frowned. 'I'm sorry, I don't understand . . .'

'It's not fair to do that,' Megan snapped. She turned her head to look at Sadie, the sudden emotion making her swallow her own words. 'To cut someone off like that . . .'

There was a depth of hurt in Megan's eyes that Sadie had not seen before. She reached out for her hand, but Megan pulled away, stared off into the shadows of the orchard. Sadie let the silence settle around Megan's agitation.

'Do you remember the boy I talked about? My first love?' Megan strung the words out, her voice lucid, careful.

'I think so . . .'

'We grew up together. Talked through the night. He was the first everything. Had this chaotic hair.'

Sadie smiled at this.

'He would read a lot, sleep late. He was always *late*.'

The strength of Megan's memories filled her voice with tears. Sadie could tell that she was seeing him in front of her.

'We would laugh at other people, know what the other was thinking. He used to really live, you know. Dance, cry, drink.'

Sadie thought about her own first love in the orchard, the startling vividness of first intimacy. Megan cleared her throat, did not try to rub the tears from her cheeks.

'We were too young, of course we were too young.' She uttered the words softly. She looked across at Sadie now. 'We grew apart and I finished it.'

Megan mouthed the words, but Sadie could not understand them.

'Megan?'

Sadie grasped her hand now, waited for her to find her voice.

'It was too late when they found him . . .'

Sadie felt Megan's hold tighten.

'He'd made sure there was no way back.'

Sadie's eyes filled with tears. 'I'm so sorry.'

'I was in counselling long enough to know it wasn't my fault. I know that. He didn't want to punish me, it's just that . . .' Megan looked down at Sadie's hand. 'I just . . . the thought of giving myself to someone after that . . . the responsibility . . . but with Jack I didn't think twice. Perhaps I should've been more careful . . .'

Megan pulled back her hand, pressed away her tears with the heels of her palms.

'Oh God, don't be careful,' Sadie said, the words running away with her, 'don't be careful.' She said the word as if it tasted unpleasant. 'I spent my life living carefully, so painfully carefully.'

Sadie shrugged. 'Perhaps I avoided a lot of pain, but I can't stop thinking about the happiness I missed out on, too. Promise me, don't do that to yourself.'

Megan's face was blotchy with tears.

Sadie wanted to comfort her, but she didn't know what more she could say.

'Come inside,' she said, pushing herself up with the cane. 'I'm sure we've got some brandy somewhere.'

51

You could not take apples; you had to wait to be given them by the tree. You would hold out your palm and curl your fingers around the fruit and, if it was ripe, the tree would give it to you. If it was not, the tree would deny you, hold on to it until it was ready. Hannah had risen early and had asked the question of the trees, and she had been given her answer. The apples were ripe, the boughs of some trees so heavy that they had begun to dip towards earth.

Megan had made breakfast and they waited in the kitchen until the morning dew had lifted, Hannah wondering silently where Jack was, knowing that they needed all the help they could get. The crop was heavy, and it would take hours to pick by hand. By mid-morning, the sun had strengthened and burnt off the last of the dew, and Hannah was satisfied that they could begin. Megan brought the ladders and Hannah found the half-barrels in the shed, stacked in a haphazard tower, and started to distribute them around the trees, lining each one with old newspaper so they would not cut the skins of the apples. Hannah handed Megan an apple apron, which she slung around her neck so that she could store apples in the pouch while working around the trees. Sadie had been forbidden from climbing any ladders, so she stood by the barrels and watched as the sun climbed higher in the sky.

Megan felt the tree giving her the apples, and she

placed them in her apron over and over, their scent surrounding her as she worked. The variety was astounding. The ones she was picking now were striped like tigers, but even then there was a difference in shape, in size, in colour, each one having taken in the sun a different way. She couldn't help but smile as she worked, the canopy of the tree providing a little shade from the sun.

She had climbed down the ladder and was tipping her haul into a barrel when she heard the van. She looked up despite herself and heard a door slam. She turned away, climbed the ladder again, and watched from the canopy as Jack walked over to the shed and fetched an apron before beginning work on the other side of the orchard. Megan tried not to be irritated by this, and carried on picking the fruit, trying not to climb down the ladder at the same time as him.

By lunchtime, a dozen half-barrels had been filled, and Sadie brought food out to a blanket in the orchard so they would not have to stop working. Megan sat down on the ground, her hairline damp with sweat, next to Hannah, who sat in her chair. They drank water and shielded their eyes from the sun as Sadie fussed in and out of the house, making sure they had enough of everything they wanted. Jack joined them eventually.

'It looks like rain,' said Hannah, turning her head in the direction of the village. There was a heavy grey cloud. 'Do you think we'll get it done?'

'I think so,' Jack replied.

'So, where have you been?' asked Sadie.

Jack tried hard not to let his eyes flick over to Megan.

'I had some work to finish, that's all.'

Sadie nodded, waiting for someone to say something.

'Well, it's a good harvest, anyway,' she replied.

Again, no one said anything, and Jack played with some grass in his fingers.

'Right, better get to work, then,' he said finally, getting up.

Sadie looked over at Megan, watching him go.

They worked through the afternoon, the sun arcing in the sky above them then eventually starting to dip to the south-west, casting shadows across Berllan-Deg. Megan's arms were aching. Jack kept toing and froing, dragging half-barrels towards the shed, conscious that it might start raining. By late afternoon, he told Hannah to go back to the house with Sadie; she was tired and he could see it, so he told her that he and Megan could manage the rest. Hannah nodded, knowing her limitations.

As the evening drew in, Megan and Jack filled the last barrels, each one aware of where the other was, trying not to get too close. As the exhaustion of the day settled upon them, Megan heard the sound of raindrops in the leaves around her. She looked up; the sky had darkened. Jack dragged the last of the barrels towards the shed, from where they would be collected in the morning.

He had dreaded coming back, knowing how she would look at him; the same slight frown, the curiosity in her eyes. If there had been any way to avoid it, he would have, but he knew they would not be able to bring in the harvest without him. He had been intensely aware of where she was all day, the mess of her brown hair and the sleeves rolled up on her forearms. She seemed always to be in his eyeline, in his space, even though the orchard was vast enough that she shouldn't have been. He dragged another barrel towards the shed. It was raining now, heavy droplets in the canopy, a terrible sadness coming over the orchard. The barrel caught in some brash and he yanked it, frustrated. He had hoped that Megan would go in with the rain, but she hadn't. She was standing waiting for him by the shed; he knew it and he tried anything he could find to keep himself busy. She just stood there, bewildered. He could see it in her.

'Are you all right?' she asked.

'Yes, of course,' he said, his voice tense.

She nodded silently.

He could feel her warmth near by. His body getting cold after the exertion. It was unbearable.

Jack closed his eyes.

'I'm so sorry,' he said. 'I shouldn't have, we shouldn't have . . .'

Megan's incomprehension was obvious.

'It's just that . . .'

'It's OK,' interjected Megan, her chin jutting out. 'I understand. There's no need to explain . . . But you're all right?'

Jack frowned, not understanding her question.

'Of course. I mean, yes, yes, I am.'

Megan stood for a moment before turning and walking back to the house.

52

W HEN HANNAH WAS A child, they used to go to
    the thanksgiving service in the chapel, Hannah
walking behind her father and mother through the falling leaves. There would be a supper afterwards in the
vestry, and the women would have spread out meat and
fruit and placed vases of late-summer flowers on every
table, which left wet circles on the white paper tablecloths. This time, and for the first time, Hannah wanted
to eat in the orchard, to give thanks there.

It had dried clear and warm after the rain a few
nights before, and Hannah and Megan had carried
out the old table beneath the trees. They had taken a
side each and navigated their way through the narrow
doorway of Berllan-Deg, Sadie watching them fretfully
every step of the way. They had placed it in the middle
of the orchard, and Hannah had stood feeling for the
first time that it was her table. She went back inside
and climbed the stairs to the old linen press, rummaged
inside for a moment, and there she found an embroi-
dered tablecloth that she and John had been given on
their marriage. It had never been used, had been kept for
best, her mother saying that it would be a pity if it were
soiled through use. Hannah carried it over the crook of
her arm and made her way back into the orchard.

She threw the cloth up by two corners and it
billowed out across the table. She then went to fetch
some wine glasses that had been kept dusty in the

bottom of the dresser. She rinsed them, wiped the cut glass clean, and carried them out, the last light of day making them sparkle. She set her table for four.

They had spent the morning cooking, boiling ham with apples and poaching pears in honey. Megan had helped and Hannah had noticed how quiet she was. Now everything was ready, they just had to wait for everyone to arrive. Hannah had even asked her guests to change. Sadie had rolled her eyes, but Megan had laughed and gone to change into an old dress of hers, putting a wool cardigan on top.

She came downstairs to find Hannah in a navy-blue dress that seemed to make her eyes come alive. Hannah smiled at her and asked her to go and put some candles on the table, directing her to the dresser where John used to keep them along with some honey jars. Megan found what she needed and took a box of matches from the top of the stove.

She carried everything outside and placed the jars on the table, putting a candle in each one and hanging a few that had string around them in the trees. She tried to light them, noticing as she did so how much of a breeze there was, even though it seemed to be still. Suddenly there was a cupped hand next to hers and she jumped, almost burning Jack with the match.

'Careful!' he said. She tried to concentrate on the flame, tried not to betray how unsteady her hand now was. He smelt of soap and woodsmoke. They moved around the candles, lighting each one and protecting the flame from the night. When they had finished, Jack pushed his hands into his pockets.

'Hello, Jack.' It was Sadie, carrying a dish of food and, to Megan's surprise, a bottle of cider.

Megan looked away.

'Be careful with that,' Jack said to Megan. 'It's dangerous stuff. Take it from me – I learnt the hard way.'

Sadie smiled.

'I just wanted to say that I can't stay; I'm off to the village.'

Sadie set down the cider, looked over at Megan.

'That's a shame,' she said evenly.

'You don't want me intruding . . .' he said. 'But thanks for the invitation.'

'You not staying?' It was Hannah, carrying more food.

'I'll see you tomorrow,' he said. Then he turned and disappeared through the orchard.

Finally, Hannah came to sit down, poured a sherry glass full of cider, and the three women began to help themselves. The orchard filled with late-summer light, golden and syrupy, and Sadie grew louder and louder with each sip of cider. She started reciting stories of Hannah's dress-sewing disasters, and Hannah told Megan the story of how, when she was around four years old, Sadie had climbed a tree and could not find a way down. Their laughter reverberated around the orchard and after they had eaten their fill, they sat back, all three drunk, not with the cider, but with the fullness around them.

Sadie raised a glass. 'To Hannah,' she said, 'who saved the old orchard.'

Hannah looked embarrassed, but smiled into her drink.

'And to the orchard that saved us,' said Megan quietly.

The sky had turned an intense blue and the constellations were shyly emerging above them.

'I don't think it was an apple, you know,' said Hannah. 'It doesn't even mention apples in the Bible.'

Sadie looked at Megan and raised her eyebrows.

'People assumed that they were apples, but they could have been figs, quinces . . .' Hannah seemed deep in thought now. 'I think perhaps it wasn't Eve stealing the fruit that scared God, either; it was the thought of what a woman could be.'

Hannah smiled and looked around the table, feeling a deep contentment she had not felt before. Then she watched as the others talked and laughed, their words seemingly getting further and further away, until the tiredness in her bones overtook her.

'Well, I think I'll leave you to it,' she said, getting up. Just then, some lights appeared on the road, the sound of an engine. A car door opening and closing. Sadie looked at Hannah, puzzled.

'I thought she'd never make it,' Hannah said, before turning and walking into Berllan-Deg.

Sadie looked across the orchard and saw the figure of Anne drawing near.

53

ANNE HAD STAYED WITH Sadie in Berllan-Deg for days while they talked. Hannah had been astounded, not by Sadie's love for Anne, but by the change in her voice, the way it had grown into itself. The defensiveness that had always been there had dissipated. She had teased Jack, walked with Anne to the village, shown her the place that had made her. Anne had thanked Hannah for retrieving Sadie's letter from the tin and posting it to her, then they had both left – Anne had some work to attend to and Sadie was going to pack up her house, ready for their return to Berllan-Deg.

This morning, Hannah sat at the table, listening as Megan also packed her things upstairs. Hannah could hear her walking back and forth. Autumn was drawing closer now; you could feel it, a certain chill in the mornings and just as the sun set. The orchard was beginning to lose its leaves, the cow parsley drying, the thistles dishevelled. A steady breeze moved gently across the window, filled with filaments, with weightless downy seeds, the plants thinking about their tomorrow.

Hannah had watched Megan withdraw into herself. Moving to the side of rooms as Sadie had once done, perceiving that the space for her was diminishing. She had come to Hannah the night before, said she would be leaving, and Hannah had tried everything she could to dissuade her but Megan was resolved to go to her old friend's house for a while, as she decided what to do next.

She heard a door close and Megan's footsteps on the stairs. Megan was standing on the last step and Hannah went to meet her.

'Are you ready?' she asked.

Megan nodded. 'I think so.'

Hannah instinctively reached out for her hand, rubbed her palm with her thumb. Megan looked down at her touch.

'You know, you don't have to go,' Hannah whispered.

Megan nodded, noticing the crack in Hannah's voice. Hannah patted the back of Megan's hand, before letting her go.

'I think it's time.' Megan shrugged, her eyes brimming with tears. 'I just wanted to thank you first.'

Hannah averted her eyes. 'There's no need to thank me.'

'There is . . . for everything.'

Megan pulled the strap of her bag further up her shoulder.

'Well, you'll always have a home here – I hope you know that,' muttered Hannah, swallowing down her tears. She rubbed Megan's arm and watched as she turned and walked towards the door.

'Just so you know,' said Hannah, clearing her throat and lifting her gaze to meet Megan's, 'forgiving him is easier because of you.'

Megan stood, her heart breaking.

'I just wanted you to know that.'

That night, Hannah walked out into the orchard and saw that Jack had lit a fire to keep away the darkness.

He kept his eyes on it as she drew near. It was a clear night, the arch of the sky cathedral-like above them. The fire had burnt through its smoke and was now pure and strong, with only a few sparks shooting up from the flames. Hannah could feel Jack's grief weighing heavily on his tongue, a bottle of cider balanced on his thigh.

'I've got a few weeks' fencing to do,' he volunteered. 'I'll come back and then be away for the winter. Will you be OK here?'

Hannah could see the tension in his face, the way his love for Megan had thrown him. She smiled.

'Of course. Anne and Sadie will be back by then.'

He kept looking at her, as if he wanted to say something, but kept changing his mind.

'She brought both of us a lot of happiness,' ventured Hannah as she pulled her cardigan tighter around her.

'Yes,' he said, his voice uncertain.

'You know, I felt so utterly betrayed when I first saw her,' Hannah confided softly, 'but she let me forgive him.'

They listened to the fire crackle. 'The thing is that we have seasons ourselves. It's so hard to grow together all the time. I don't think the world lets us. That doesn't mean there's no love.'

Jack let the words settle on him. Considered them.

'And we just missed each other; we so very nearly loved each other properly.'

Jack looked up at her, had never heard Hannah speak so openly before.

'I miss his voice,' she said, before laughing.

Jack watched the warmth of the firelight on Hannah's face.

'You know he always whispered to me? The first time was in the library, the first day I met him. We were whispering and the librarian just scowled at us. He made a face at her, making me laugh even more.'

Jack smiled now.

'And then, when he moved in here, he'd mouth rude things behind my mother's back.' Hannah's face was soft with remembrance. 'The desperate whispers on the phone, when we lost . . .' Her smile faded now. 'When we had the miscarriages . . .' She was staring at the fire, her eyes dark with tears. 'And then, in his last days, I would press my ear to his mouth to hear what he was saying. Our love was woven from whispers, and you know what?'

Jack could hardly breathe.

'I have felt closer to him in his death than I did in life. I have come to understand him more.' Hannah laughed sadly. 'We so *very* nearly knew each other, loved each other properly.'

She was nodding now, a grief-stricken smile.

'There's a time to act and a time to speak. Don't make the same mistakes, Jack,' she said, getting to her feet, and, as she did, she pulled a bundle of letters from her pocket and offered them to him. 'I think John would have liked you to read these,' she said.

'What are they?' questioned Jack.

'His legacy.'

Jack took the letters, glanced at them.

'They're in Welsh,' he said.

'I think you'll understand,' Hannah answered, and Jack watched as she made her way back to the house. Then, in the light of the fire, he unfolded them, and he read about John and Hannah's long years of apples and honey.

54

Wax

*At the end of the nest, just as at the beginning, there is
no pollen, no brood, no honey, no eggs. There is only
wax, creamy and matte, a beautiful subtle golden
shade. It is a colour that does not draw attention
to itself; it is not brazen, it is opaque and milky
and made for light. The finest candles are made of
beeswax, and their luminosity is unparalleled. The
flame is clean, honest, does not smoke. The most
wonderful thing, though, Hannah, is that its light
is not harsh, it does not cast dark shadows, it glows
with a purity that is breath-taking.*

*I'm dying, Hannah, and the light that you have
given me will comfort me on my way into this
darkness. I cannot say that I am scared, but I am sad
to be leaving you in this way. My heart is no different
to any other dying heart, wondering why it was sent
here to beat, but one thing comforts me. People die,
but love does not. My love for you is apart from me,
it is apart from my body; it exists outside of me and
in you. I hope it will exist in the orchard, and I hope
it will be there in the language of the bees. Nothing
I have done is worth anything, and the one thing I
should have done well I failed at. The light tells me
that now. And I can see with clarity, with a piercing
simplicity, how this short life fooled me into thinking
it was long, how it pressed its complexities upon me*

when I only had one simple thing to do. If you cannot forgive me, Hannah, then give my love away. Give it to Jack, to the orchard, give it to someone, to anyone; remember me not for me, but in loving them.

55

THERE HAD BEEN A few weeks of milder weather, a glowing incandescent second summer. The morning mists would dissipate, leaving the orchard in sharp focus. The shadows were getting longer, indicating that winter was on its way, but the warmth clung on regardless. The trees were shedding their bronzed leaves and the evenings brought with them a certain exquisite stillness.

Hannah found she slept heavily and woke in the mornings feeling rested. She would still let her palm travel to his side of the bed out of habit, but then, on finding it empty, she would lie on, watching the orchard she had cultivated through the low windows. Afterwards, she would walk downstairs, open the old door and watch as the soft light suffused the kitchen. Her appetite had increased, too, what with the washing of the trees for their winter rest and gathering wood for the fire. She would toast some bread, slather it in honey and lick her fingers as it ran luxuriously from the warm bread down her hand.

Her mornings were filled with wrapping cooking apples in newspaper to place in the shed for storage, with the boiling of elderberries for syrup, and with reading; her afternoons with the expansion of her plans for the orchard. Her orchard was more new than old now, and so she had ordered some books, ledgers that she had made significant progress in filling. She had drawn a line under her father's records and started anew. She had also drawn a new map, showing the families of trees, with notes and dates of planting. Under the dates she had detailed the next twenty years of progress, allowing, of course, for nature to make its own plans, too. She would add to these daily, building up her legacy, securing her succession.

As Hannah had hoped, Jack had disappeared from the orchard and, a few days later, he had returned with Megan. Hannah had been tasting this year's honey, dipping a spoon into the jar, when she had heard their footsteps on the worn slate doorstep. They were entwined, Megan's face emanating a subtle luminosity and Jack's a deep calmness that came from entrusting themselves to each other. They told her that they had spoken about John's letters, teased out their own meaning, and, after drinking tea with Hannah, they had retreated to the caravan, their laughter occasionally carrying through the orchard, reminding Hannah of John.

It would also soon be time to put the hives to sleep and she had asked them to do that – they were theirs now. They would have to interpret the language of the bees, understand their ways, and Jack said he had plans to construct some new hives, too, made to his own design. Hannah had assured him that John would have liked that. The warm weather of the last few weeks had seen the bees still flying, gathering stores, the lengthening of the season a good indication that they might make it through another winter.

It had taken Hannah a few weeks to rearrange the parlour, too; she had painted the walls, hung some pictures that she liked. She had brought in more lamps, more cushions, and she would leave the windows open, letting in the light and air. Now she would often eat her breakfast there, leaving the door to the kitchen permanently open.

In the evenings, Hannah would spend the last of the light sitting in the orchard. She had never really done that before, had never had the leisure just to sit – there had always been something to do – but these days, she could think of nothing she wanted to do more than sit and listen to the trees, her skin warming in the sun, and, if she was still, she would merge with the sounds of the orchard so that she was hardly there.

There were three harvests in the Bible, her father used to say, and there were three in the orchard, too. The first was honey, the second the apples, the third would come soon enough. She drew her father close to her now in her thoughts – his face, his dark eyes, and the way he would sit, his hands in his pockets, at the beginning of a story – and she found herself forgiving his weakness, his human frailty. His inability to come to her. If she closed her eyes, she could still hear the fruits swelling, filling their skins, their colour deepening and their flavour sweetening. Her mother came to her, too; her childish pride, her blue eyes that had seen too little. Even John – he would come sometimes; she would see the warmth of his eyes or hear him whispering in her ear. Face after face would appear to her, and she would feel a displacement, a kind of longing that belonged to someone separated from a world they once knew, from the time that made them.

She had thought, too, that her body seemed to be merging with the trees, the veins on the back of her hands becoming prominent, root-like, the white of her hair like the blossom, and they filled her dreams once again; not dark and black now, but full of light. She would lie awake at night in semi-consciousness and be with them, among the mosses, the lichens, the worlds within, and she could feel the heaviness of the fruit in her body and the heartbreaking tenuousness of the stalk.

Acknowledgements

I HAVE BEEN INFATUATED with bees for a very long time but fell firmly in love with them when I learnt that some old hives were shaped like books. I was entranced with the idea that their world and ours could meet between the covers of a novel. I am deeply thankful therefore to Wil Griffiths and Lewis Gruffudd for teaching me to open that first hive over a decade ago and am grateful that they still share their wealth of experience when I am at a loss. My heartfelt thanks also to my brilliant and astute editor, Kirsty Dunseath, whose genius lies in the lightness of her touch and the sharpness of her eye. Thanks also to Alice Youell who so graciously started the editing journey on this book before her career move. I would also like to acknowledge the hive of people at Doubleday who work incredibly hard to give each book the attention it deserves and whose passion for books is so uplifting. As always, I would like to thank Anwen Hooson, my agent and friend, who greets my every, sometimes intense, obsession with equanimity, encouragement and humour. I will forever be trying to elicit the tone of voice you use which tells me you think something is working. Last but never least my thanks to my wonderful family, who keep me sane and drive me to distraction in equal, wonderful measure.

About the Author

Caryl Lewis is a multi-award-winning Welsh novelist, children's writer, playwright and screenwriter. Her breakthrough novel *Martha, Jac a Sianco* is widely regarded as a modern classic of Welsh literature and sits on the Welsh curriculum. The film adaptation – with a screenplay by Caryl herself – won six Welsh BAFTAs. Her other screenwriting work includes BBC/S4C thrillers *Hinterland* and *Hidden*. In 2023, she won the Wales Book of the Year Award for the third time for her debut English novel *Drift*, making her the first writer ever to have won in both languages. She is a visiting lecturer in Creative Writing at Cardiff University and lives with her family on a farm near Aberystwyth.